SHATTERED
by
DEATH

A Jo Oliver Thriller
Book Two

PRAISE FOR CATHERINE FINGER'S

AWARD-WINNING
SHATTERED by DEATH

A modern day Ten Little Indians by Agatha Christie, Shattered by Death is a rollercoaster of twists and turns that will lead you to a heart-stopping end. Catherine Finger is proving to be an author to note as up and coming.

—**Sandra Brannan**, author of the *Liv Bergen Suspense Series*

Shattered by Death captivated me from page one! Finger weaves together a page-turning novel that follows Detective Josie's path on a chilling murder mystery where Josie quickly becomes one of the main suspects that jeopardizes her path to adoptive motherhood. As a forensics expert and crime drama writer, I found Finger's investigative details accurate and entertaining! Elegant, intriguing and suspenseful storytelling. Settle in with cup of coffee and enjoy this ride!

—**Jennifer Dornbush**, screenwriter, speaker, forensics maven, and author of *Forensic Speak: How to Write Realistic Crime Drama*s

In *Shattered by Death*, Catherine Finger takes us on a page-turning tale that keeps us riveted from beginning to end. With a crisp, clean writing style, Finger has crafted characters that stay with us long after we've finished the book. I can't wait for another release from this stellar author, who has just joined my favorite writers' list.

—**Kathi Macias**, author of more than fifty books, including Golden Scrolls 2011 Novel of the Year, *Red Ink*

Coming from a law enforcement family, I especially enjoyed Shattered By Death. But anyone and everyone would love this intense, suspenseful novel that pulls you in from the very beginning and keeps you enthralled until the last word. I'm so glad this is part of a series. I'm hooked!

—**Kathy Collard Miller**, speaker and author of many books including *Never Ever Be the Same*

SHATTERED
by DEATH

A Jo Oliver Thriller

Book Two

Catherine Finger

 Elk Lake
PUBLISHING, INC.

Plymouth, Massachusetts

Cover Design: Derinda Babcock
Interior Design: Derinda Babcock
Editors: Erynn Newman, Deb Haggerty

PUBLISHED BY: Elk Lake Publishing, Inc., 35 Dogwood Dr., Plymouth, MA 02360

Library Cataloging Data
Names: Finger, Catherine (Catherine Finger)
Shattered by Death, A Jo Oliver Thriller, Book Two / Catherine Finger
220 p. 23cm × 15cm (9in × 6 in.)
Description:
Identifiers: ISBN-13: 978-1-948888-05-9 (trade) | 978-1-948888-06-6 (POD) | 978-1-948888-07-3 (e-book.)
Key Words: suspense, murder, police, detective, relationships, adoption, divorce
LCCN: 2018941256 Fiction

DEDICATION

This one's for you, Mom.

ACKNOWLEDGMENTS

Thank you to my dear friends and family members standing behind me and joining me for the journey of the Jo Oliver Thriller series. Special thanks to Jodie and Carl for serving as my super human character studies as Josie's world continues to turn.

Sincerest thanks as always go out to my readers. This second book in the series was a given—especially after hearing your questions and hopes for Josie, Samantha, Nick, and our other new friends. I'm certain I've delighted some of you and frustrated others—all in my quest to tell a good story. Thank you for hanging in there with me and offering suggestions along the way.

CHAPTER ONE

Wednesday, March 23

My legs rolled out a rhythm of their own, commanding cross-country skis into one smooth glide after another through the quiet evening snow. A full moon glistened overhead. Samantha gave a happy cheer behind me, and I answered her with a girlish squeal of my own. My cheeks quivered with the force of the smile pouring across my face. I steered around a sharp corner and bent down into the wind, grabbing the snow with the tips of my poles to propel myself even faster down a short, steep hill. I slid to a stop and turned to watch Samantha's descent.

I cupped my hands and yelled encouragement to my little bundle of spunky joy. "Alright now! You go, girl!"

She was a natural athlete. If everything went right, and she was living with me full-time before June, I'd have to ask around to see if there were any camps I could enroll her in for the summer. She'd hate that, but camp was a battle I was going to win. Just not tonight. Tonight, we had the luxury of brilliant stars, a spectacular moon, and the noisy creatures of a perfect Wisconsin winter all to ourselves. Let the magic continue. Lord knew Samantha needed some magic in her life.

Her little legs pumped hard, netting her an impressive burst of unnecessary speed.

"Slow down, girl! You're gonna wipe out!"

I was new at all this and was beset with worry over the slightest things. What would a regular mom do? *Is this normal? Do little kids take corners on cross-country skis at breakneck speed? Are you supposed to sit there and watch them as they flirt with danger, propelling themselves to a certain and gruesome death? How does the rest of the world even do this every day?*

"Watch me, Josie! Watch me!"

I gasped as she leaned into the corner and flew gracefully down the hill. She was heading toward me at a pretty good clip, and there was only one set of tracks forged into fresh powder. Milliseconds before careening into me, she jumped sideways, both skis aloft, stopping on the snow beside me.

Who taught her all that? She was a natural. I was going to have to find something more challenging than the four walls and three members of her current foster home between now and The Day if I was going to have any chance at all of harnessing her resilient, playful spirit.

"Josie?" Her face was aflame with happiness, and she wasn't winded at all.

"Yes, darling?" My eyes teared up as I looked at her.

"It's just that, well …"

Whatever fears swirled within, she was trying hard to share with me. Would I be successful at helping her banish them?

"Is this about the court appearance next Thursday, sweetie?" She was nervous about the review. Heck, my own stomach was full of butterflies. We were about to go in front of a judge who had the power to declare something God had already whispered, boomed, and burned into my heart: Samantha was my daughter. There were just a few more legal hurdles to clear in the adoption process.

What was she afraid of? Did she know something I didn't?

Lamb's eyes moistened. She stared at me, fidgeting in silence.

I stepped out of my skis and knelt beside her, sinking an inch or two into the snow, until I connected with the earth. I would do anything to be that solid earth, that sense of safety, that strong foundation, for her. *Lord God, pour out Your solid love through my hands, to her heart.*

"I love you, Samantha. I know this is scary … and wonderful at the same time. And I feel it too. Mostly what I feel is so very happy to have you in my life and to get to be your mom." I kissed her cheek and drew her into a hug. Breathing in her beauty was my elixir. *Thank you, Mighty God. Thank you for my little miracle.*

Her little arms wrapped around my sides, and I almost missed the gift of her fear revealed. "My forever mom?"

"Yes, darling. Your forever mom."

We finished the last half-mile of the trail side by side. I smiled up at the sky and thanked God for bringing this amazing child into my life. The Paradise County Department of Children and Family Services sponsored weekly outings for foster students and their families. With the adoption less than a month away, my heart fluttered at the thought of being able to bring Sam home to our house. This was one of the last times I'd have to watch her board a bus and head back to her foster "brothers and sisters."

I followed the bus back to Haversport, flashing the squad lights every now and then just to give Sam another reason to smile on the way home. The beauty of our time together carried me through the evening. Tomorrow morning's schedule included what would no doubt be an unpleasant attorney conference call. One more mile to go before I sleep—and awaken to the new world of full-time motherhood.

CHAPTER TWO

Thursday, March 24

"Josephine, I'm sorry, but you married a bad man. A very bad man."
Andy's voice whined over the phone. "I'm sorry. I don't know what else
to say."

I dragged my hand through my hair and gritted my teeth. Andy had
been recommended as a divorce attorney with both brains and heart. It
was important to me to be able to look back one day and not be ashamed
of myself for falling into any crazy behavior. Over the years as a small
town police chief, I'd seen enough of what people could turn into during
the final throes of a bitter divorce. I'd wanted a divorce attorney with a
conscience, one who could protect my interests—both financially and
ethically. Now all I was getting was soaked. Daily. *Be careful what you
wish for*.

"Now what's the creep want?"

"You won't want to hear this." He lowered his pitch to a more or less
tolerable level.

"Yeah, so? What else is new? Hit me." I clicked the envelope icon on
my computer. My email snapped open.

"That's an unfortunate choice of words. He *is* hitting you. He's hitting
you up for another forty thousand dollars." He rattled the last phrase off
as if he'd planned to drop the words and run.

My stomach clenched, and I curled my palm around a ceramic mug
on my desktop, soaking in the warmth of the coffee within. Squeaks
and groans slipped out from my grinding teeth. "I don't have another
forty grand. I don't have another forty bucks. You know that. I'm sick
of getting pushed around. Tell the he-vamp *no*."

"Josephine …" Exasperation whiffled through Andy's voice. He
disapproved of the way I referred to my soon-to-be-ex-husband, Del,
and his also-married-to-someone-else girlfriend. What did he want from
me, a cutesy little Hollywood couple mash-up? Delamra? Too civilized.
The he-vamp was genteel enough. I shuddered. I'd broken my own

rule of never thinking of both of their names at the same time. *Good riddance. Tamra can have him. I guess.*

"He's already taken everything. My marriage, our lake house, half of the equity in the house I'm sitting in, the remainder of which won't be enough to pay for this phone call, and every last cent I have. And now he wants me to play dead and fork over another forty grand? He can go scratch."

I clicked an email at random. It was the verse of the day. John 12:25 popped up, the King James Version no less. I opened a browser and looked the verse up in a different translation. "Whoever loves his life loses it, and whoever hates his life in this world will keep it for eternal life." *Good grief. At this rate, I won't make it to life eternal. I can't afford it.* The Scripture was a good reminder of my recently acquired relationship with the One Most High, though. *I'm sorry, God. I know I'm being a putz. I know I should tone it down a bit. I'm trying to be a better woman, trying to take the high road.* Whatever that was. *Amen?*

Reality burst through my awkward prayers. But forty grand? Where would I even begin to come up with that kind of money? My gaze settled on a wooden frame showcasing the three people I cared most about. My eighty-year-old mother sitting on a bench at the edge of the dock next to Samantha, the two of them looking frail but happy. A sun-kissed Italian man stood behind them, one arm draped around each of their shoulders, leaning down as if he were about to share the secret of the century with the women he loved.

"Listen to me. We're almost through this. You're moving on to bigger and better things, remember? Keep your eyes on the prize." Andy was on a roll. An expensive roll.

"What does that even mean anymore?"

"Samantha. It means we've got to keep doing everything we can to keep you squeaky clean in front of the judge and, God forbid, in front of the court if we have to go down that road. Which I'm still hoping we won't."

Samantha. Balm of Gilead to my soul. I pictured her flying down the little hill on her pink skis, framed in last night's moon. "Alright. What do you suggest?"

"I'm sorry, but you're going to have to give up this last little bit of money—and you do have it. It's the exact amount of equity left untouched if you were to refinance your house."

"Gah! He *knew* that! He's just doing this 'cause he can. Can't you stop this freight train? What do I pay you for?" I stopped and took a deep breath. *Dear God, forgive me for being a self-centered jerk.* "I'm not going down without a fight. Can't you spend a little more time on case law or something? Get me outta this mess with a little bit of my dignity left intact?"

"We're not interested in his motivation. We're interested in one thing: closure. Being done. So you can move on with your wonderful new life."

"Okay, fine. Do it. If this is really what it's gonna take, I'll call my bank today. Just get through this as quickly as possible so we can move forward with the adoption process. I surrender."

"You forgot the best part."

"So *Samantha* can start a new life with a new family. With me."

I ended the call before I started either swearing or crying. *What if I can't handle being a mom?* My shoulders tightened and pain snapped across my temples. *I don't know what I don't know.* I squeezed my eyes shut, breathing rapidly. *What if I'm horrible at this?* My heart beat wildly, and I started to tremble.

Warmth descended upon me, feathery blankets of golden mist seemed to settle around me, lifting my spirit. In my mind's eye, a brilliant light emanated from the center of the golden mist, surrounding me with overpowering sense of love and peace. I smiled, opened my eyes, and leaned into the Presence I could not see. My Magnificent Being stood with me like a golden warrior, enveloping me in His love. His voice called out a truth I'd read in a recent devotional. "Faithful is He who calls you, and He also will bring it to pass." I opened my eyes and watched as the mist evaporated, burning away my fear, and leaving me with an ocean of peace.

CHAPTER THREE

Thursday, March 24

Even after basking in the presence of my Magnificent Being, the conversation with Andy had still left me jangly and raw. My feet pounded the jogging path as I rounded the corner toward home, tree branches drooping low overhead and remnants of the morning's mist shrouding a dark shape on the ground ahead of me. A smarter woman would have slowed down, maybe stopped. I poured on the speed. I hadn't had a run this smoothly for days.

The closer I came, the bigger the form appeared until I realized, too late, it was a log. *Stop? Speed up?* I hustled and leapt over the log like I was born for it, resuming my steady pace with a triumphant smile.

I made my way over the winding gravel path leading to my back porch from the miles of trails that wove between my subdivision and the nearby forest preserve. Ten pounds wasn't all I'd lost in the past few months. Four months ago, a huge log like that would've caused me to turn back—head down, dejected. I liked the new me.

A tree wasn't the only obstacle in my way lately. Maybe it was time to leap over them all. There was one last confrontation looming as the final date of the divorce decree drew near like a thunderstorm on the horizon. I owed it to myself to go and give my soon-to-be-ex-husband and his younger, sportier model, the piece of my mind I'd been holding back for months out of courtesy and self-respect and okay, maybe a little fear. *Courtesy?* I leapt over courtesy long ago, along with that big ol' log. I left it all behind me in the dirt.

I rooted through my jacket pocket and pulled out my key. A pink sticky note floated to the ground. A verse from Malachi written in Gino's block print. "But for you who fear My name, the sun of righteousness shall rise with healing in its wings. You will shall go out leaping like calves from the stall." Oh, brother. While I had already forgotten my vow to work harder on becoming a better woman, Someone else had not.

Fine. Between God and Gino, my dear friend and guide to all things spiritually-related, I was bound to become that better woman soon. Time to redirect my thinking.

Today is the first day of the rest of your life. Start it right... with no regrets. No righter way to start the day than an impromptu visit with Samantha. There were only a few days of Spring Break left. Maybe I'd pick her up, and together, we'd surprise my mom with dark chocolates and brunch. Three generations of Oliver women in one spot. It doesn't get much better than that. I hummed as I walked through my house and headed for the shower. Ten minutes later, I was dressed and moisturizing.

I'd call Sam's social worker and foster mom to get the okay to pick her up in a few hours. First, I had another stop to make. I was going to take my final ride down that beautiful lane to my old lake house, knock on the door, skip the drama, and get my holiday china. We were speeding into Easter, and I wanted my alabaster rabbit and my lamb cake mold, so I could have my Easter back, on the way to getting my life back.

And I'd have them by sundown. Just one more log to leap over today.

I headed out to the highway, scenes from the marriage that had left me behind floating all around me, until a drain opened in my mind, sucking them all down the big black hole of loss that had become my personal life. I flipped the blinker on and pulled into the lake house's subdivision for the very last time.

Today, I'd say goodbye and truly stop looking back. But not without my holiday china.

CHAPTER FOUR

Thursday, March 24

Fueled by visions of my famous Easter vanilla-almond lamb cake, complete with rich white buttercream frosting and the requisite coconut fleece, I picked my way through the streets leading to my lake house. My mind clung to the symbol of the resurrection. An Easter morning cross, adorned with an artfully hung purple robe, stuck in a mound of Easter grass—bright greens and pinks, littered with jellybeans, chocolate bunnies, and peanut butter eggs.

Five minutes later, I nosed my car up the asphalt driveway curving gracefully to the McMansion I'd bought for my husband to enjoy with my replacement. Viburnum, heavy with buds, lined the entrance. I wouldn't get to see them in full bloom. I glided to a stop next to the back porch steps, noting my expensive electric car standing at attention in the driveway. I moved to the driver's side window, and peered in. Another woman's jacket hung carelessly on the back of the passenger-side headrest. A fistful of rocks lurched through my stomach.

The car sat squarely in front of the first garage door. It was open, so they were probably inside. *What to do? Ring the doorbell? Front door? Back door?* I wasn't company, but I sure wasn't family. I steeled myself and sashayed right through the garage to the back door like I owned the place. Because heck, I still did own the place.

I rapped on the door. Silence. I knocked again—louder—three times in a row, bracing myself for the clack of mincing, four-inch-stiletto-clad footsteps on my hardwood floors. The pitter-patter of my marriage walking out the door of no return.

Nothing.

I retreated down the steps and walked out of the garage in slow, measured steps. *I know they're here. They must be ...* Fresh air breezed across my face as I looked down the hill at the boat house on the edge of the lake. Mist steamed off the water. In some alternate universe, Del and I might have been sitting at the end of that dock, drinking coffee, greeting the new day together. But that world had only existed in my fantasies.

I should offer a quick prayer. *But what if God doesn't really want me here? Better to keep Him out of this right now. I'll pray later. God might not be as invested in getting back my holiday china as I am.* I took a few deep breaths and headed to the boathouse. *Sorry, God. We'll talk later.*

At the bottom of the hill, a shudder ran through me, forging iron posts where my feet had been. Shivers jiggled up and down my spine, and the hair on my arms spiked up. I headed toward the water. A few months ago, I had walked out onto the dock with Del. He, laden with a fragrant bag of pastries, walked with one arm too firmly wrapped around me. I, for one mad moment, was stiff with the certainty that he wanted to shove me into the icy waters. How had I not seen the end of my marriage coming? *And where was God when I needed Him? Why hadn't He stepped in and stopped the destruction?*

Reaching the bench, I thumped down on it. How stupidly proud of this bench he'd once been, and of how he'd "requisitioned" it from the city. *What's the difference between 'requisition' and stealing, Del?*

Can't you just shut it, Jo? Or are you going to ruin another day in paradise for me?

We see what we want to see. I sat a moment longer. If this bench could have taken me back to the way things were, would I have stayed seated? Or would I have been strong enough to get up, move, and find my own path forward?

I jumped up and walked to the boathouse. Over-sized porthole windows flanked the doors facing the lake. Someone had moved a large storage cabinet in front of one of the windows. A piece of dark cloth hung crookedly inside the other. *Odd.*

The heavy plank doors hung open several inches. Were Del and Tamra inside? Gentle splashing against the dock, the breeze flowing through the river birch, and morning birds all sounded in the early spring air. No noise came from within the shed. What were they doing, if they were in there? *Do I really want to know?*

I conjured up the image of my porcelain soup tureen, with its hand-painted tulips and violets adorning the edges and smooth, white, rabbit-shaped handle. Andy'd made it clear I had to ask for the few remaining things I really wanted back, and that's exactly what I was going to do.

Ask permission. A streak of fire raged through me. I shook my head to extinguish it.

I closed to a few feet from the boathouse door. Something was very wrong. Dizziness rolled over me as an assault of thick smells wafted out between the heavy doors. I braced my feet, willing myself to stop moving forward. Even though the scents were repulsive, I leaned in.

I could reach out and touch the doors. Every fiber of my being screamed *don't.* I leaned in a little further. Until it hit. An odiferous attack—a tangy metallic mixed up with mildew, turpentine, rust, and earthworms.

There was the telltale buzzing. I put my hand on the door handle, creaking it open several more inches. The buzzing gave way for a moment. Positioned within five feet of the door, as if it were pointing, was a bloody deck shoe.

I followed the line of the shoe to the edge of a dark red pool of blood—the way to my husband and his lover, holding each other closer in death than he and I had ever been in life. Then, I ran out of breath. I was screaming at the top of my lungs.

I clenched my hand over my mouth, backed away from the boathouse, turned, and threw up.

Automatically, I pulled out my work cell and hit 9-1-1. "This is Haversport Chief of Police Jo Oliver, calling from my home at 1020 Loon Drive in Wauconda. Reporting a double homicide. Of my husband and his mistress. I found them on the floor of my boathouse on Bangs Lake."

Dispatch asked rapid-fire questions, words floating around me, dreamlike.

"… double homicide … your husband, ma'am?"

"Yes, my husband and his mistress."

"Ma'am?"

"Officer Del Reed. And his girlfriend. Send out teams *stat.*"

I hung up while she was asking me to stay on the line, scrolling through pictures to find Nick's chiseled features, his flawless olive skin. I pressed my thumb against his cheek and waited for the solid comfort of his voice in my ear. *Please be here for me again, Nick.*

He answered on the first ring. "Hello, beautiful."

"Nick …"

"What's wrong?"

This man who knew me so well would sense the tremble in my voice that no one else could hear. "Nick! I need you. Come. Please, just come. Now.

"Where are you? I'm on my way."

"I'm at the boathouse."

"The boathouse? Why?"

"They're dead. Both of them."

"Dead? Del?"

"Yes."

"Both of them?"

"Yes."

"The girlfriend?"

"Yes!"

"Just stay put. I'll be there in ten minutes. Have you called it in?"

"Yes, just before I called you."

"Don't touch anything. Don't move. I'll be right there."

I clung to Nick's voice like a lifeline. The best of the best the FBI had to offer—a man I might have married in another time and place. I needed all the power that Nick Vitarello could rain down on any crime scene in the United States with just one phone call.

If I ever needed you, I need you now.

CHAPTER FIVE

Thursday, March 24

I'd promised not to touch anything. I'd promised to wait. The combination of throwing up and calling it in had cleared my head, and I had just under ten minutes to soak it all in. I started taking pictures with my cell phone. The open door. Snap. The layout of the bodies. Tamra's body lay broken. Snap. A gunshot wound to Del's right knee. Their knee caps? Snap.

Del. I pocketed my phone. My hand fell limp at my side. I stepped near his head and looked down, my gut clenching. His mouth was drawn into a sickly smile. I leaned down a little lower. Fishhooks pulled his lips up on either side into a gruesome, impossibly cruel grimace, fishing line knotted behind his head. His eyes were wide open in horror. His chest looked crushed in, right above the heart. What was left of his broken body was too horrible to contemplate. Whatever else might have happened was impossible to tell.

Given the nauseating smell, coupled with the level of decomp, these bodies had been here at least a day.

Tamra was a shattered doll, arms and legs sprawling. She'd been placed in Del's arms, with one leg draped across him, but the leg was broken and twisted. Where her hip should be, the fabric lay in the wrong direction, dried blood everywhere. The back of her skull was crushed: dried blood, gray matter, and who-knows-what had oozed out all over the wooden boards underneath them. I looked away.

It was off. Crime techs would figure this out, but there weren't blood spatters everywhere. Why not?

Del … *dead?* My feet might float into the air. *Dear God, I'm sorry. I'm so sorry, but in some secret place of my soul I'm a little relieved.* They were sprawled across the boathouse floor. My boathouse floor.

They got what they deserved.

This would not look good for me at all. If I had been sent to investigate this murder, would I ever have believed in the innocence of a soon-to-be-former spouse just happening to arrive first at the scene and conveniently all alone? Nope. Not on your life.

I was in a boatload of trouble.

A silent scream formed on my lips as tires crunched on the gravel drive. I stepped out of the boathouse. Nick's sedan raced down the hill toward me. He braked hard at the bottom, sending gravel everywhere, sliding the last few feet to a stop. When he stepped out, three men got out with him. I'd raised the level of threat and investigation from county to federal with just one phone call. The locals wouldn't like that. But I needed Nick by my side, running this thing down. *Sorry, God. I know I should be leaning on You, but right now I'm turning to Nick.* I needed a little more work in the trusting God over man department.

His men fanned out to secure the scene while he bee lined over to me and put his arms around me, claiming me with one warm embrace. I sighed into him, unable to speak, clinging to my life raft. Whiskers brushed the top of my head as he swiveled his neck, taking in the scene before him. We stood like that for a long minute. Then, he pulled away and gently turned me around. We walked together to the end of the dock and sat on the bench. He produced a small bottle of water and two aspirin.

"Take this, beautiful." He pressed the aspirin into my hand.

I swished the water around my mouth, spit it out, and downed the aspirin.

He pulled his phone out and turned on the recorder app. "Tell me everything."

I leaned into him and recounted the day's events for the first time. My words echoed through the fog of my daze as sirens screamed in the background. Half a dozen cars from around the county pulled up while I spoke. The men Nick had brought with him assumed command and began telling the locals what to do. This was not going to go well. Too bad.

I clung to my lifeline. *Shouldn't I be clinging to a different Lifeline? Sorry, God.*

Paradise Sheriff Deputy Grundy arrived. He was not my friend. Bulbous nose, gut like a fitness ball gone slack—he didn't walk—he waddled down the path. The pressure of his appreciable weight shifted the pylons as he made his way over the wooden dock to us. A sneak attack it wasn't.

"Mind telling me exactly what happened here, Josephine?" His sneer was less pleasant than usual.

On any other day, I'd have made him refer to me by title. Today was not any other day.

Nick stepped in front of Grundy, shielding me from the larger man, invoking nature channel scenes of lions and rhinos in Africa. In a battle pitting the stealth of a lion against the bulk of a rhino, who would win? I shuddered. What was Nick going to say or do that could possibly make a difference now?

"Deputy. You'll find everything you need from Chief Oliver right here." He held up his cellphone. "I've just sent the recording to your work email. The Chief's had enough for one day. I'm taking her away from the crime scene now. You know where to reach her."

I should say something, but nothing came. Thoughts flitted around like frenzied bats, but my tongue was a cold, marble slab. *Do something. Say something. Defend yourself.*

I stood in silence. Eyes not focusing on anything. Shapes and colors drifting in and out. Voices blending together.

Grundy was bellowing on about something important, but I couldn't make it out. My husband's body lay just feet away from me, but I couldn't draw my thoughts to remember where. He wasn't alone. And I couldn't think about why. I couldn't think about anything.

I walked next to Nick, his arm around my shoulders, through a cluster of men wearing badges, hats, and scowls. I trained my eyes on the ground, kept my feet in synch with Nick's footsteps. Even as we walked in unison, I knew I was relying on man for a security only God could give.

When we reached Nick's car, he opened the door and tucked me into the passenger seat like a porcelain doll. He slid in the driver's side, ignoring the stares and murmurings of the cops surrounding us. He reversed up the hill to the end of the driveway and turned toward Haversport.

We'd gone about half way before Nick pulled into a used car dealership off Highway 120 and parked among the inventory. He turned the car off, reached for my hand, and focused all attention on me.

The force of his stunning brown eyes hit me full on. "Josie, Del's murder is a terrible tragedy. I need you to understand that his death will not be your investigation. I'm taking you home. That's where you need to be right now."

"No. No way. That's the *last* place I want to be. We're going back to the station. Work. I need to be at work. Besides, my car's still at … I want to…" I had no idea what I wanted. But I liked not facing this alone.

"I'm taking you home, sweetheart. And then I'm going to call Donna, and I'm going to go to your station and start sorting things out. Mitch and I will get your car home later today. And bring you a warm meal. I just need you to know why I'm taking you home right now. This isn't up for debate." He turned away from me, pushed the start button, and pulled back onto the highway.

We drove in silence, a tight leaden ball in my stomach. Exhaustion whittled away at me. I closed my eyes and took a deep breath.

"I really don't know what to do next." I lay back against the headrest.

He picked up my hand and drew it to his lips, delivering a whisper-soft kiss. "Nobody ever really does, beautiful."

CHAPTER SIX

Thursday, March 24

Nick pulled into my driveway and was at my car door before I unfastened my seatbelt. My uncoordinated hands pawed at the buckle. Slow motion snippets of the crime scene rolled over and over in my mind. Investigators would be combing every inch of my lake property now. What else would they find?

"Beautiful?" He was standing at my side with the door open. He'd been talking, and I'd missed every word.

I nodded and heaved myself out of the car. We walked up the porch steps together. I fished my keys out of my pocket and fumbled with the door, dropped the keys. Nick picked them up, opened the door, and placed a hand on the small of my back, ushering me in.

"Josie. It's going to be alright. Everything's going to be alright. I promise you we'll get the guy who did this. In the meantime, I need to know you're safe." He pulled me against his chest, and I stood in the foyer, leaning into him, arms limp at my side. "Stay here while I go in and see what we've learned so far. Unless you'd rather I stay?"

I shook my head, clinging to the sound of his voice, letting it roll over me like a prayer. We stood there, wrapped together, for several more seconds, the warmth of his body purring into mine. I pulled away and looked up at him.

"I think I need to be alone. I need a little time to think this through. And you need to go do your thing. Go, get this investigation started. I'm alright. Really." If he stayed here much longer, I wouldn't be able to think of anything else but the comfort and safety of his arms. And we both had a lot more to think about right now. "Go. I mean it. Get to the station. See what the guys have come up with. Keep me in the loop. I'll be here. For now." I pushed away from him, setting my jaw.

"I got your back. Always. We'll get this guy. I'll check in every hour or so. Promise me you'll text if you need me?" His brown eyes softened. The light in the foyer reflected green flecks as he looked down at me.

"I promise. Now go."

Then I turned him around and closed the door behind him.

He paused for a moment, putting his hand on the glass, spreading his fingers out wide. I matched my palm to his over the cool glass. He was going to end up visiting me in prison. I snatched my hand back and waved him away.

Nick's presence on the other side of the door dissolved into a faint smattering of footsteps and distant car noises. Images of Del and The Other Woman—even in death I couldn't bring myself to say her name—darkened my mind.

Dead. *Del is dead.*

And so is … so is *she*.

Pulling myself away from the door and treading into the kitchen took an impossible load of energy. I plugged in the electric kettle and prepared some peppermint tea. While it was steeping, I sat in front of the four large windows facing the small lake in front of my home. Gray-white fog swirled and danced over the water, waves shimmering through the haze. Little white gulls plunged down to the surface of the lake, snapping back up with their prey.

Between the haze in my mind and the swirling mists, I almost expected a dorsal fin to pop up at any time. Blood-soaked jaws of an angry shark swam through the concrete floor of the boat house in my mind. I shook my head and refocused on the landscape in front of me.

Two huge pine trees perched like sentinels on an embankment overlooking the water. One was solid green, its companion littered with brown patches. Something must've been eating it alive. Killing my tree. River birch swayed in wide arcs, delicate leaves and branches tossing and turning next to thick swaths of sumac. Dead leaves swirled up high enough to pass through branches weighted down with new buds.

I wrapped both hands around my mug of tea for warmth. A fire would be nice. But I'd have to get up and make it happen. Not yet. Remnants of zebra grass blew back and forth next to blackened coneflowers I hadn't gotten around to cutting back last fall. What kind of woman would let her beds go untended? The kind of woman men left for other women who didn't? My rose bushes stood out in defiance against a backdrop of soft green lilacs that would be blooming in less than a month. Where would I be by the time my roses were in full bloom?

After a hot shower and pouring myself another cup of tea, I stood in my bathrobe at the kitchen window, drowsy and lost. I rummaged through three cabinets and the freezer, but the cotton in my head only thickened. I trudged upstairs and dropped onto my bed.

The buzzing in my bathrobe pocket grew louder as I shook the sleep from my eyes. I stretched my arms over my head, pulled myself out of bed, and grabbed the phone.

"Oliver."

"Thank God! I've been calling and texting you for hours. Why is your car in the driveway and why aren't you at work?" Donna's soothing tones coaxed me back to life.

"You need to sit down, Donna."

She remained silent until I made it through my gruesome morning discovery. "Oh, Josie! I'm coming over."

"No. You're not. Please. I need a few minutes alone. Just let me get dressed, sort myself out, and I'll text you to come by."

"Promise?" The warmth in her voice buoyed me.

"Promise." I ended the call, dressed, and headed downstairs.

Time to put on a pot of some serious coffee. I'd need it to help me think and feel through everything I'd just experienced. From home, in front of a soon-to-be roaring fire. Safe. Had my husband and his girlfriend really just been murdered? What kind of God would allow this? How could this be happening? And what would happen next? Shivers danced up and down my arms.

I stared at the wood piled in a basket next to the fireplace. I rummaged around in the basket, finding long matches, kindling, and waxy pinecones that would add color to the flames. Now all I needed to do was open the flue.

I bent down, leaned over the grate, and felt along the rough brick interior, searching with my fingertips for the cold metal handle. Finding it, I pulled hard. Nothing. I bent deeper at the knees, bracing my left hand against the brick to give me more leverage, and pushed, opening the flue wide. My knuckles hit something hard and cold, but my fingers were still wrapped around the steel handle.

What the ...?

I pulled my hand out and ran to the kitchen junk drawer for a flashlight. Four long steps, and I was back on my knees on the brick hearth, pointing the flashlight up into the inky darkness.

A sledgehammer was jammed between the flue handle and the chimney wall.

I gasped and jumped, bumping my head against the brick and dropping the flashlight, which went out. I felt around for it in the dark. *Gotcha!* My hands wrapped around the plastic, and I took a deep breath and looked up again. The handle of the sledgehammer was mottled with dark stains. I inched the light up the handle to the iron hammer. Blood.

I pulled myself out of the hearth and sat back on my heels. White noise filled my head. My bones were heavy and cold. Thoughts jumbled about like bits of fruit swimming through an ocean of Jell-O, dancing and jiggling but never quite connecting. How long had that *thing* been in my fireplace? Was that the weapon that killed my husband? When had the killer placed it there? How did he know where I lived, and how did he get in and out without me noticing? And most of all, *why?* Why was he framing me?

My thighs were burning. I set the flashlight down and heaved myself to my feet. I found my phone in my purse and searched for Nick's face again.

"Babe?" His voice was quiet and solid.

"The fireplace, my fireplace … there's a murder weapon in it. Maybe." The woman in me warred with the cop in me. I needed the cop to surface. Fast.

"I'm heading over. Did you touch it?" He was always in cop mode. His tone gave nothing away.

"I … I'm not sure. Part of me did. Just my knuckles though, I think." Did I touch it beyond that first brush?

"Whoever planted it there would've been smart enough not to leave prints. Let's keep it as pristine as possible. Ever seen it before?"

"I don't know." Del had had a sledgehammer, hadn't he?

"We'll sort it out later. Why don't you call this in and get a forensics team on the way?"

"Yeah. Good. That's good." It was good, wasn't it?

My practically-ex-husband and his girlfriend had been found murdered on our lake property just a few hours ago. And then what must have been the murder weapon had turned up in my fireplace. Anyone with half a brain would know that I had plenty to gain by the untimely death of my husband in the middle of our divorce proceedings.

Whoever was behind this was in possession of a devilish yet brilliant mind. No one was going to look better as the prime suspect than me.

CHAPTER SEVEN

Thursday, March 24

A bloody sledgehammer planted in my fireplace. Maybe this time I was up against something too big for me to solve on my own. Thank God for Nick. What would I do without him? Hummingbird wings fluttered in my chest.

For the second time in the same day, I was trembling, waiting for Nick. *To do what, save me?* More bird wings beating in my heart. Did I need saving?

Del and, and *his other woman*, murdered.

Maybe I did. The beautiful creature blurred to a stop, wings merging into one large, veined leaf, with its own rhythmic swaying.

Why couldn't I manage my life on my own? Was my new life going to include being managed by other people? *I don't think so.*

Steel walls slammed down between my heart and my head. What kind of woman was I turning out to be? The veined leaf bent under the growing weight of the hummingbird. *I didn't need Del, and I don't need Nick. I can't live my life clinging from man to man, like Jane of the jungle in search of her next Tarzan.* Stormy winds ripped the leaf apart, replacing its warmth with a steel ball inside my chest.

Three short raps on the front door windowpane interrupted my ruminations. I shook my head once and rose to let Nick in. I'd grapple with the feeling of my life being in his hands later. I was no one's damsel in distress. Not even Nick's.

He walked in, his crime scene go-bag clenched in his right hand, half-hugging me with his other arm. "Show me, beautiful."

I pointed to the hearth. He'd built more fires in it than I had during the past few months. *He could have easily planted the sledgehammer.*

He walked past me to the great room, stopping to set his case down on the coffee table. Hesitating, he looked up at me. "Okay if I spread out here?"

"Of course. Let me help you clear it." I swooped in, moving cooking magazines and my mug of cold peppermint tea. Isolation cascaded down around me as he walked right by without reaching out to touch me. Was I invisible to him now?

He pulled out his tools, put on his gloves, knelt down, and started snapping pictures with his phone. "So aren't you going to ask me why I'm here?"

I cocked my head at him. A travel-sized can of luminol sat on the floor next to him. "Uh, 'cause I called you?"

His jagged smile almost reached his eyes. "And because I've officially taken this one over for the good guys."

He still didn't seem very happy to see me. *Avoiding me out of guilt?*

"That good news or bad news?" That he could get permission this quick to have the Feds take over this case didn't surprise me. That he found it necessary to do so, did.

"Good news. Always and only good news when it involves you and me, beautiful." He set up a small light in the hearth, switched his phone to video. A faint blue glow emerged.

He spoke into his voice recorder. "Having arrived and entered the house, I am now in the suspect's chimney, with a visual on a potential murder weapon."

His voice was matter of fact, Joe Friday.

Suspect? Heat flashed over me. *Is he taking over the case so he can bury any evidence that could clear me?*

"There is a large, wood-handled sledgehammer stuck between the steel flue and the brick sides of the chimney. The iron head is mottled, possibly with dried blood, as is the handle. The crime scene techs will be dusting for prints next." He switched off the light and reached for his phone to push the video off and pocket it. He squirmed out of the chimney, sat up, and looked at me.

"I know it's upsetting, hearing me making it official like this. But it's the best way—keep every procedure clean to protect the connection between us." His phone buzzed. He paused, read the text, and looked up at me, frowning.

"What is it?" *What else could go wrong in my life right now?*

He was pensive, lips pursed. "That was Mitch. One very angry Corey Richardson, husband of Tamra, was just brought in for questioning."

Blood drained from my face, my pulse slowed down. "The husband?"

Nick nodded. "Routine."

"Do you need to get to the station?"

He shook his head. "I want to position myself in the best possible way to make sure I can stay close to you and monitor this nightmare investigation up close and personally." His eyes softened, moistened.

He was trying to protect me. At least, I hoped he was. Assuming he wasn't trying to frame me. I should've been grateful. He needed me to respond, needed to know I was okay, but I had needed *him* not to get right to it. Not to go for the evidence first, not to turn right into Johnny-on-the-spot Super Cop. *Why the rush?* I could think of nothing to say. I stared back at him.

"So we're going to preempt all suspicions by following procedure every step of the way, getting the crime scene boys here to do what they do best. And yes, maybe I'm going overboard, treating you as I would any other suspect …" His eyes were glistening now.

"But I'm not any other suspect." My voice was cold.

"I can already tell you that's blood on the head and the handle." He cocked an eyebrow to the coffee table, to the now-darkened black light.

"Yeah. I was here when it glowed, remember?" Anger and exhaustion were at war in my tone. "What's next?"

"We're going to wait for the locals to arrive. Make sure the crime scene techs get started, expedite it. And then you're going to continue to cooperate one hundred percent. It's the only way."

Silence filled the space between us.

A thousand pithy comebacks floated through my mind. I willed any one of them to come to my aid, to break the silence. "What is that even going to look like?"

Not very snappy.

Nick sighed, stepping nearer. "It'll look like me at your side. Us going to the station together. Sharing the evidence and giving your deputies the decision-making power over you and trusting whatever it is they come up with."

"They'll arrest me. This kind of evidence? They'll arrest me for sure." I threw my hands up in the air, gave my head an angry shake, and stepped back to increase the distance between us. "It's what I would do. Somebody walks into my office with this kind of irrefutable evidence, no matter who they are, I'm gonna cuff their butt and toss 'em in jail— at least for a night. Give them some time to think about it while their attorney starts the clock."

"That's what *you* would do. That might not be what Mitch decides to do." His tone carried an air of confidence. Almost as if he were suggesting he knew my people better than I did. He was wrong about that.

But, as for how Mitch would to respond to my sorry plight? He was right. Commander Lauren Mitchell had been with me for all five years I'd been Chief of Police in Haversport, Illinois. I promoted her twice, as much for her expertise as for her wisdom and compassion. I had at least a fifty-fifty chance of not spending the night in jail with Mitch sitting in my judgment seat. Pretty good odds, considering.

A crime scene technician knocked on my front door.

"Okay." I picked my purse up off the counter.

"Okay, what exactly?" He finished packing up his gear and snapped his briefcase shut.

"Shut up and take me to your leader. Before I change my mind." I grabbed a black trench coat from the hall closet and walked to the front door, Nick's hurried footsteps echoing behind me.

CHAPTER EIGHT

Thursday, March 24

After Nick got the tech team pointed in the right direction, we drove to the station in silence. My right hand was gripping the handle above the passenger door so hard I could've popped a bicep muscle. Inhaling deeply, I relaxed my hand, one finger at a time. "Are we there yet?"

Nick snorted. "Welcome back. I thought I'd lost you for good. And just in time, too."

He eased into my station's parking lot and pulled into a visitor's slot near the entrance.

"You do get that this is a lot harder on me than it is on you, right?" Was I joking with him or flirting? How many hours after finding my husband's mutilated body? Sometimes I defied even my own low expectations of myself.

"Great. Looks like we've got company. At this hour? What is it, after eleven? Coming up on midnight?" Nick stared at the foyer, tsking in disgust. Several dark shapes clustered near the door, faces all but pressed up against the glass. Someone pulled out a cell phone and pointed right at our car.

"Think the camera still adds ten pounds?" I got out of the car and headed to the bottom of the steps to wait for Nick.

"Doesn't matter, beautiful. It all looks great on you." He put a hand on my shoulder.

Was he trying to comfort or control me as we ascended the steps in front of the gathering crowd?

I looked up into the foyer. Liz and Mitch stood in front of a small horde of cops and assorted people of the night. The tallest one grunted something at the others, jabbing his head in my direction, wolfish grin widening as he looked at me. Schlichting, my least favorite cop, already reveling in my distress. *Figures.* A balding guy sporting what looked like media credentials pointed a distressingly large camera at me. *Old school.*

"Breathe, beautiful. Just breathe. And follow me." Nick took the stairs ahead of me. I followed behind, mustering as much dignity as I could.

"Un-frickin-believable." I muttered at my salivating colleagues. News of my pending arrest must've spread like blood in the waters. *Creeps*. I scanned the crowd. Which of my thirty-seven colleagues would be counted for me, which against me?

Mitch pushed the door open, nodding grimly at me. "Chief."

"Mitch." Ribbons of molten lava hardened in my throat.

Indistinct sounds bounced off the walls as we passed through the parted group of uniforms. Flashes illuminated me. Would the lighting show off my cheekbones or the dark puffs of color pooling underneath each eye? Nick took hold of my arm. I floated beside him, watching the surrealistic march from a corner of the room, near the ceiling-mounted security camera.

Mitch appeared from behind us and pushed open the door that led away from our office suites. To the interrogation rooms. *Great.*

She stopped at the largest room and ushered us in, then closed the door and walked away, her heels echoing down the hall. The three-hundred-square-foot room was cleaner than usual, faint smells of bleach and antiseptic lingering in the dense air. The requisite rectangular, wooden table sat in the center, two chairs set up on one side, one chair with a notebook, pen, and tape recorder in front of it on the other. And three unopened bottles of water.

We sat in silence for about thirty minutes before the door opened, and Mitch stepped inside.

Mitch looked at me, doubt swimming with sorrow in her green eyes. She nodded at us. She couldn't believe I killed Del and his girlfriend, could she?

A thousand things to say flitted through my mind. None of them seemed right. I opted for silence. Her show. Her opening move.

"Chief, we need to go through some of the basics. You understand." Her bravado melted away. More sorrow than disbelief floated in her eyes now.

"You should have everything you need. Did you read the transcript from the boat house?" Nick had come alive, inserted himself.

"Yes." Mitch was back to her professional self.

"And by now you'll have dusted the weapon for prints?" Nick's narration was getting on my nerves.

"Yes." Mitch turned her gaze to the one-way mirror.

Guarded good news. Come to think of it, the fact that I was sitting in an interrogation room, and not a jail cell, was also relatively positive. Why hadn't I been arrested? They must not have found enough hard evidence. Corey Richardson had also been brought in for questioning. Classic. Take a close look at the spouses. I shook my head, and turned my attention back to what was going on outside of my head for a change.

"So, there's no real reason for you to be questioning the chief, is there?"

Nick had something up his sleeve. We both knew I wasn't guilty, but what else did he know?

"Other than the fact that her husband and his girlfriend were brutally murdered on the eve of her costly divorce, and what is very likely the murder weapon happens to show up in her fireplace, you mean?" Mitch was going for sarcasm, but fell short, ending up with a bit of a whine.

"Your guys narrow down the window of death?"

If Nick was asking, it was because he already knew this answer too. The decomp of the bodies in my own rudimentary examination would've put the time of death somewhere in the past day and a half to two days—not much more than that. Was he trying to establish an alibi for me?

He wouldn't be able to come up with one. There wasn't one—at least not one I'd ever share. My whereabouts during that time would remain off limits. Other than my sacred few hours of play time with Sam, I was screwed in the alibi department.

An awkward silence filled the room. Nick fidgeted. He put his left hand over mine on the table—in front of Mitch—in front of God and everybody sitting behind that wall of glass in front of us.

I snatched my hand away from his. Apprehension snaked through me. "What is it?"

Nick picked up the water bottle in front of him with open palms and rolled it. Slightly to the left, back to the right. Then he set it back down and looked at me. His eyes glistened, and deep awareness burned my bewilderment away, leaving anger in its place.

"Don't do this. It's not worth it. And you do *not* have my permission."

He knew. He must have known and, somehow, he must have come up with proof of where I'd been. "You have no right. This is my decision. Not yours."

"No, not any more it isn't. Not when your job, your *freedom* is on the line." He fished in his pocket. "Not when I have your own personal get-out-of-jail-free card." He pulled his hand out of his pocket and pressed it into my palm.

My fingers found hard edges, flat sides. I closed my hand around the little object and shut my eyes, offered an unintelligible prayer for wisdom, for protection. Then I opened my eyes and unclenched my fist to reveal the flash drive Nick had given me.

"Doubtless this will detail my whereabouts during the past twenty-four hours." Rage settled into my gut, swirling, pulling anything not nailed down into its angry vortex.

"More like forty-eight. And I'm confident that Mitch knows how to handle a piece of evidence confidentially." Nick-speak for *no one needs to know what's on it—where you've been.*

I narrowed my eyes. "I'll give it up, but only if I retain the right to recant later if something goes haywire and we end up in court."

Mitch coughed, paused for a long minute, giving me enough thinking time to realize something key.

I let out a long breath. "It's inadmissible anyway. Evidence obtained illegally."

"Useful in making a determination of sufficient evidence of non-involvement." Mitch arched her brows, and she reached out her hand for the flash drive. "Not that we'd need more of an alibi than your time with Sam, but you know me boss, I'm all belt and suspenders, just like you taught me."

"But still, I need your word that the identities of these women will remain hidden. Or I'm not giving up the drive." Even as the words escaped my lips, everything clicked together. The look that passed between them was confirmation. "But you don't even really need this, do you? Ten to one, copies of this drive have already been emailed to you, right?"

Mitch's face reddened.

Nick stared into the middle distance.

My volunteer work spanned three different women's shelters in two counties. Each of the facilities had top-of-the-line security systems, including cameras in every public space, over every entrance and exit. Once a month, I took over round-the-clock supervision duties so the director could get a much-needed break. One of the shelters catered to a very well-heeled population. The kind of women no one would ever believe would be in need of protective services.

I placed the flash drive in Mitch's outstretched hand.

I turned to Nick, the tightness in my gut relaxing. Maybe he really was trying to help. "You get all this done in between my calls?"

"I had help."

CHAPTER 9

Thursday, March 24

Gino!

I looked up at the one-way glass, rage building inside me. "Gino, why don't you come betray me face-to-face?"

Mitch glanced into the mirror and nodded. Thirty seconds later, the door opened, and Gino stepped inside. His bulky, six-foot frame looked cartoonish under his red do rag. His olive brown skin paled when he caught the anger boiling out of my eyes at him.

He put his hands up, as if warding off blows. "*M'hija*, you must believe me. It was the most prudent move."

"Jeopardizing the safety of the women in my care isn't something you get to make decisions about, Gino. How dare you? How dare any of you? This should have been my call." And they knew that. So why had they gone over my head? Colluded? Unless maybe someone didn't believe in my innocence?

"It won't get out, Chief. We'll see to that. Your women will be safe with us." Mitch was already putting the drive into a small laptop she'd had retrieved from a briefcase under her chair. Her movements were crisp, full of hope.

"You shouldn't have needed to go this far, Mitch. You shouldn't have had to wonder about it." I wasn't being fair. They'd found a potential murder weapon in my home, after I happened upon two dead bodies. Any normal person would've wondered about it. A little, right? Though I wasn't sure I would've. I tend to be pretty loyal to the people on my team. Turns out, my loyalty maybe wasn't going to be reciprocated.

"She was just doing her job, m'hija."

"Maybe so. But you've known me what, over ten years? After all we've been through, you're not rock solid enough to talk these jokers out of violating the identity of the women in my care?"

Mitch had the drive in and the computer whirring. All heads turned at the sound, as if a magical answer would pop up at any moment and clear my good name.

"I not only did not talk them out of it, but I suggested this might be the fastest way to prove your innocence beyond a shadow of a doubt, as I knew very well where you had been. And I also knew that this electronic proof would allow us not to have to rely on the testimony of any of the women in your care." Gino's chocolaty eyes sparked.

He had a good point. Maybe I should calm down, start seeing this as a good thing. "I'm sorry. I just don't like all of you going behind my back, treating me like a suspect. You could've just talked to me. Some Good Friday this is turning out to be. Guess I'm in good company, you know, what with being betrayed by my closest friends and all …"

Someone snorted from the hallway, and a low murmuring began. *What the …?* Liz, my administrative assistant, poked her head in, nodded at me and pulled the door shut. I could hear her shooing all the guys away. No doubt this gruesome case was about to become the greatest show on Earth—right here in our little town of Haversport.

"Whatever you're about to see on that screen is no different than what you already know to be true about me." I sighed, stretching out my arms, loosening tension from my shoulders to my wrists. *But it is going to change what I thought I knew about each of you.*

Mitch, Gino, and Nick—three of my best friends in the world—sat huddled around Mitch's laptop across the table from me, like a clan of hunter-gatherers congregating around a fire. Their feral expressions left no doubt about their intent. They would find evidence to prove my whereabouts during the timeframe of my husband's murder, or they would arrest me on the spot.

Ice pumped through my veins. Would I ever be able to trust them again? How far had news spread of the murders and of my submitting to a midnight rendezvous for a special round of questioning? And what was going on with Mr. Richardson? The walls of the interrogation room were all I had between me and an increasingly hostile world.

Judging from the voices in the hallway, off-duty cops had been called in to deal with the aftermath of the double homicide. And no matter which way the evidence ultimately shook out … some of them would believe the worst of me from here on in. The tenuous thread of respect I'd fought so hard to earn, and struggled to maintain, from some of the staunchest of my old school colleagues, would be severed tonight. Unless we got lucky. Fast.

"*Alli esta.*" Gino's voice snapped me back to the present.

The three of them leaned in to the computer screen like little kids looking up theme park tickets online for their parents.

"Unmistakable." Mitch was jotting notes on a pad next to her computer as she scrolled down her screen. "Assuming you didn't pay some hack to kill him, to kill *them*." Eyes lowered, she cracked a grim smile as they reviewed security footage from my last shifts at the women's shelters. "Don't worry, we'll investigate every angle."

"Sometimes I hate you guys." I pushed my chair away from the table, crossed my arms, and stared at them. They were doing their job. *Then why had Mitch morphed into Judas before my eyes?*

"What do you expect us to do? Stand by and let you be arrested? Not gonna happen. Not on my watch." Nick met my stare, rocking back on his heels, away from the computer screen.

"These women come here …" I pointed to the computer screen. "… to me, because they know I'll protect them. That my word is my bond. Up until tonight, they had reason to believe me when I said no one would ever know they had come to our haven. I promised them safety. I don't like the feel of this." My mind raced down a path including a messy murder trial.

"M'hija," Gino's voice was tentative. "We know your heart beats for these women and so does our own. We can redact any identifying information and make sure that anyone needing to view this as proof of your innocence does it only in sealed chambers, and in the presence of an officer of the court. You can trust us in this, and in another more sensitive matter." He looked from Mitch to Nick. Nervous?

"Another matter?" I stared at him.

"I am … we are thinking, it might be best …" His trailing off made it even harder for me to pay attention to him. My wandering mind conjured a scenario in which Nick, Mitch, or Gino might be compelled to release the tapes as a way of documenting my innocence and justifying my non-arrest.

"For you to, ah …" Gino hesitated again.

It sounded as if he were talking through water in a barrel. I couldn't concentrate on what he was saying. Had the identities of the women who had come to me for safety, for shelter, already been compromised? The room was starting to blur. I placed my palm on the edge of the table to steady myself. Bottom line: Mitch wasn't convinced of my innocence. Not one hundred percent.

"… after surrendering your weapon …" Mitch had picked up the baton from Gino, doing her best to spell things out. "… taking care of things for the next week or so …"

I rubbed my eyes. Those women had trusted me. Something I'd have never relinquished had now been stripped from me and offered up. Their safety was being exchanged for my freedom. A sacrifice I wasn't worthy of.

"… agree not to return to duty until being examined and released by Dr. Kira Stoklavich." Mitch stopped talking and stood up.

"Oh, no, I'm not wasting any more of my time with that crazy hack." Wasn't anybody on my side anymore?

"Think of it as less about you, and more about keeping all options open." Mitch had one hand on her hip. Ready for a fight? Would she ever fully trust me again?

"I've got my rights, my freedom." My inner sixth grader made an appearance. I was gearing up to give them a piece of my mind. And Mitch could go hang if she was ready to bail on me already.

But what if remaining free was a condition of me staying in the clear to adopt Samantha?

"Okay." I slid to my feet in acquiescence.

We stood around the table for several seconds in an awkward standoff. A tremor moved up Mitch's leg, and she pulled her eyes away from mine. "It'll only be for a few days, Chief. Gonna do you a world of good to get out of here. Take care of yourself. Get away from this insanity." She fixed her eyes just over my shoulder. Was there someone else on the other side of that mirror?

"'Cause there won't be any insanity when I get home?" I willed her to look at me.

It didn't work. "Nick'll be there with you—for you." Her eyes swept from the glass to Nick and back again.

"No, he won't." I didn't need a handler.

"Gino then." She cocked an eyebrow at my Cuban ally.

"Nope. I'm gonna go home alone. Catch a little quality time with Sam and, with any luck at all, my mom. Wait this crap out together. Lay low." I held up my hand. "Any objections?"

The three of them stared at me in silence. They watched while I pulled out my Glock, and laid it on the table. Mitch stared at the floor, fidgeting.

Nick coughed. I stripped off my holster, and snapped my badge out of my purse and dropped them into Gino's outstretched hands.

"You know where to find me, amigos." I nodded once before marching out of the room and down the hall without another word to anyone.

CHAPTER TEN

Friday, March 25

It was close to one in the morning by the time I piled into a taxi, and headed home. Shadows wrapped around the buildings I passed almost every day of my life, lending an air of unfamiliarity to the streets of Haversport. Twice, I caught myself nodding off as we drove through the abandoned night. I let out a long sigh as soon as the car pulled into my driveway. After tipping the driver, I dragged my weary body through my house and up the stairs and fell into bed.

In my dreams, I was a beautiful, tiara-clad princess, dressed in white. I faced the beauty of a new day, watching the sun's first light bouncing off smooth-sided mountains—reflecting my fully redeemed image. I was a princess, daughter of the King of Kings. Then I felt a little tug, like a child pulling on the top of my crown. Curious, I looked up, toward the glossy mountain.

A bolt of lightning struck at my feet—shockwaves rippling through my body. Clouds ripped open from heaven, and a booming voiced called down to me. *Run! Run! Run!*

Primal fear charged through me and I tried to flee, but my feet were stuck in quicksand.

I awoke to light pouring in my windows. My heart was pumping a million gallons an hour. Hot and cold sensations flowed through me.

I lay still in bed for several long minutes, piecing the dream together. Deep breaths helped slow down my heartbeat. There had been a message behind the dream, and I fought to bring it back into the light long enough for me to catch it. A veil opened, and the message surfaced.

Run! Run! Run!

After nearly ten years behind the badge, I'd learned to trust my gut. My husband had been murdered alongside his girlfriend—just months after I'd learned he even had a girlfriend. Any remaining sense of personal safety shredded with the dimming fragments of the dream.

Run! Run! Run! Was my spirit trying to tell me something? Was I in danger too? I threw off the covers and picked up my cell phone off the nightstand.

Several texts peered at me. Three from Nick, two from Mitch, and one with an attachment—an unknown number. I scrolled down and opened the attachment, ignoring the growing sound of alarm bells somewhere in my mind.

The text was an odd emoticon sandwich. A winking smiley face sat on the first line, followed by a link to a media site. Another smiley face was at the bottom of the text. This one crying a river out of both eyes. The look of the thing gave me the creeps.

I shrugged it off and opened the link. Today's headline and byline shouted at me. "Local Chief's Husband and Mistress Murdered During Bitter Divorce." The article went on to say, "An unknown source in the Paradise County judicial system calls the murders 'suspiciously convenient.'"

Was this how people would see me now? If this early morning media campaign was any indication of what was to come, my job was on the line. From the looks of the article, and the string of nasty comments that followed, doubt had taken seed overnight and grown in the hearts and minds of colleagues and community members alike.

A new text came in as I stared at the screen, sender "unknown." Cold fingers tapped up my spine. The muscles in my arms went rigid.

Don't feel so bad. They deserved it.

Gasping, I dropped the phone.

I stood in the morning sunlight, shaking in my pajamas. Was this some sort of misplaced benevolence? Or was this a message from the killer?

I forwarded both sets of texts to Nick and Mitch. For a moment, I grappled with which one to call first. Could I still trust Nick?

Nick Vitarello had been in my life longer than I cared to admit. Our tempestuous past included a tangle of professional and personal experiences that had created an unbreakable bond between us. But that was before I'd been set up for murder, and called him in to help. Had he helped? Or had I unwittingly helped *him*? Could any relationship survive *that*?

I hovered over Nick's picture several seconds before pressing my thumb on Mitch's face instead.

Mitch answered on the first ring. We talked about the texts first, speculating on whether or not they'd come from the killer. She listened to my thoughts, her nimble fingers tapping keyboards over the phone. "You'll never hear this from me, but Richardson is one angry hombre."

Her words floated over me. "What? Did something happen during his interview?"

"Guy's got a rap sheet that'll curdle fresh milk." The tapping stopped. "Assault is the most frequent offender. Recent, too. Looks to me like this wasn't Tamra's first rodeo."

"What are you saying?" *They deserved it.* "You saying Richardson sent that text?"

"I'm saying we don't know what we don't know. He could have. He's the type. But for now, I'm ordering phone taps on your cell and work phones, and getting a tech on your texts."

Richardson. My unlikely ally, or a jealous spouse turned murderer? I pushed the thought out of my mind. I had more immediate concerns. "Thanks. And while you're busy playing good cop, I'm taking a short walk on the other side of the street."

Mitch gasped.

Rather than reassure her, I took advantage of her stunned silence to ask for a huge and inappropriate favor. "I've got to take a look at the evidence."

She didn't say a word.

Goosebumps shivered over me. Cool beads of sweat ringed my forehead. We had to get to bottom of this now—before the killer had time to surprise us again. Since I was out of the office by mutual agreement, the evidence lockers were off limits too. Maybe a little walking tour with the phone on speaker as she itemized the evidence was something Mitch could do for me. I took her silence as reluctance. Just a step away from full support.

She took over a minute to answer. "I can't let you do that. Not until you're cleared."

"Right, but just hear me out." I waited for her approval.

"Go on." She exhaled.

"So, what if you just happened to read the report out loud to me? You know, like you were practicing for, I don't know, court or something, and accidentally purse dialed me?"

"I can't *describe* the stuff for you. That's not that different from letting you into the lockers. That won't work. It's playing with fire." Her cadence shifted. She wanted to help.

"What do you mean you can't describe the stuff for me? Of course you can. It's not like I'm going to record you. All I need is an idea of what you've got so far." To win her over, I balanced my commanding phone presence with a mild whine.

The voice that could soothe the savage beast ramped it up a notch as Mitch pushed back. "Chief, you know you can't do that. Nobody involved in a crime, directly or indirectly, can get access. Not even you."

Heat rose up the back of my neck. "If I wanted your opinion—"

"You just *asked* for it." I could almost feel the impatient stamp of her rounded one-inch heel against the concrete floor. A faint echo rimmed each word as she clipped down the hall toward the evidence lockers. *I was winning.*

"I'll be a good girl, keep a low profile. I won't even drive by the office until I'm cleared to return—you've got to trust me. Doesn't our friendship deserve a little trip down evidence locker lane with you?"

"No. Probably not."

"*Probably* not?"

"Definitely not."

"What if I have probable cause?"

"You probably don't." Mitch let out a long breath. "This is hard on all of us. I've never been in this situation before. I want to do what's right for you, for me, for the department, for the case. You've been given a bye on being hauled back in on the wrong side of the law anytime soon, but your innocence hasn't yet been proven beyond a shadow of a doubt."

She was dead on the money. What had happened to innocent until proven guilty? The truth of this horrible case was a long way from being unearthed. Only two people knew that I was innocent: the killer and me.

Don't feel so bad. They deserved it. Even if the texts had come from the killer, what good did they do? I didn't have enough to prove my innocence to the media. At least I had Mitch on my side.

Her footsteps had grown silent. The murder weapon should have been tagged and stored by now. *Murder weapon.* The muscles at the base of my neck tightened.

"Look—it's my funeral. I can't stand another minute of wondering what you really know for sure and what you think you know. The tension is killing me over here!" There were other ways for me to get

44

at this information—legal ways—but I wasn't done imposing on our friendship. And acting like her boss. While I still *was* her boss.

She didn't deserve to have me shouting at her. She wasn't the one in trouble. I was. She was only doing her job—just like I taught her.

It wasn't Mitch's fault my lowlife husband had cheated on me with some woman half my age and then taken a virtual knife to my throat in court via his equally lowlife attorney. Nor was it her fault someone had taken a blunt instrument to his cranium before he could complete the process—rendering him and his girlfriend extremely dead and leaving me extremely guilty-looking. Kind of a trifecta if you looked at it from the killer's point of view.

And once we caught said killer, I planned to ask him all about it. Images of the crime scene bubbled up inside me. Betrayal could get your blood boiling, I knew that. But had it spurred the man to a double homicide?

"I'm sorry. Let's regroup. How about you leave your phone out by accident and switch it to a video call for me as you stroll around the room? That can't be against any rules. That way we don't even have to talk about it. We're not talking, and we're not texting. No witnesses. Never happened." I was pushing it. But screw it. I was playing centerfield in a murder investigation, and I didn't like standing up alone in the heat.

"Always wanted to be a member of AV club in high school and never quite made it." Mitch resumed her even strides.

"And why not? Your talent behind the camera is legend." I wasn't just buttering her up. She had the eye. Her YouTube videos had earned hundreds of thousands of views.

"The cop wannabes were way hotter than the AV geeks in high school, so I went the cop route instead. No regrets." She ended the call and, within seconds, had sent me a five second video starting and ending with artistic shots of the not-so-shiny black and white tiled floor leading to the evidence. She was just about in.

It's good to be queen. Usually. But today it was way better being Chief of Police.

CHAPTER ELEVEN

Friday, March 25

"We need to hire a better cleaning service. That floor should be black and white, not black and yellow." I couldn't help the color commentary.

Mitch was talking me through her tour of terror in the bowels of the station via a video call. I was packing for a morning workout at the gym, followed by a quick visit to Samantha, as we talked. Might as well do something useful with my forced hiatus. I'd be able to keep Mitch on the phone more or less alone until the morning shift change began in a few minutes.

The camera took in more yellowed tile as she walked down the hall and stood in front of the solid steel evidence room door. A round mirror was mounted above the door. Mitch's slender figure reflected back at me as she held one hand up, pointing the phone into the mirror.

"And you need to gain a few pounds so I can hate you just a little less. There some new ordinance against body fat you've neglected to mention, or did you win another month's worth of low-carb diet bars? You got no hips, woman. It's unnatural." I doubled my resolve to take full advantage of my time off. On any given day, it was even odds whether or not I could snap my gun belt around my waist, let alone let it ride down cool and low on my hips, like Mitch's.

"You should get out more, Chief—lots of action on the other side of the desk. Great for fat burning. Not that you need it. But keep in mind, the camera adds ten pounds, so ..." She was laughing now.

I loved her laughter. Hearing it again in the midst of the long, dark night of the soul that my life had suddenly become was like listening to a special concerto of Liszt and Elton John featuring dueling pianos. Minus the Vegas fanfare.

"Yeah, I get it. You're even hotter in person. I know. I see you every day in polyester pants, remember?" I took in the familiar scene as she walked through the door. Her footsteps sounded gritty against the cement floor.

"Well, watch me walk over to the third shelving unit." She held her phone up and narrated as she walked.

"We know the perp had at least two weapons—three if you count whatever drug they used." Mitch's steps slowed.

"*What?*" The new information kept piling up.

"Suspected use of some kind of drug. A definite needle mark was identified on both bodies a few hours ago by the ME. The shoulder of one, and the palm of the hand on the other. We're working on tox screens now, but whatever it was it gave the killer plenty of time to do his worst. Slow things down, give him a chance to enjoy the show." Mitch's shaking hands kept the camera bobbing up and down as she scanned the evidence boxes.

"At least our perp used a gun. A small mercy maybe?" Her voice betrayed her struggle to maintain her composure and finish this gruesome task.

"I thought you said it wasn't a shooting." Invisible fingers crushed the soft flesh under my chin. My brows shot up.

"No, I said it wasn't a *fatal* shooting."

Tiny beads of sweat dampened my forehead. I closed my eyes, fishing for anything to say to lighten the mood and pull my attention away from this horrible death at the hands of a mad man. Even Del didn't deserve this.

"Don't make me paint the scene for you, Mitch." My jaw ached. I unclenched my teeth.

"Make up your mind. Are we breaking this down together or not? What about your 'less is more' axiom?" Mitch moved the camera along the shelf of tagged evidence boxes and bags.

"Oh, brother. I don't know any more. This is a lot to take in. Did you get a sense from the ME of the length of time it took for them to go? Lie to me if you have to … please tell me their death wasn't as horrific as the scene suggested." I had to stop, cradle my head between my hands. My living room was spinning.

"It's pretty nasty." She stifled a gagging sound as she spun the camera back to the evidence bay. Focusing in on the shelf, she passed the bags and pulled a large evidence storage box to the floor. Setting the lid aside, she zeroed in on a see-through tube sporting a hypodermic needle.

"Is that the killer's drug kit?" It couldn't be anything else.

"Check." Her voice had quieted to just above a whisper.

Asking the questions, sticking to the facts, helped ease the tension in my body.

She followed my lead, kept acting more like a cop, less like a person who'd just lost a former colleague.

"Where are the other two weapons? And why use three when two would do?"

"Better safe than sorry. This was a careful killer. He—or she—she wanted them dead, really dead."

"But why the belt and suspenders? Why use a gun when you have a disabling drug?"

"Because he needed to buy himself some time? Maybe he wasn't very strong? The surprise factor would only last a few seconds. He shot them in the legs first and then got close enough to drug them. He must've been pretty good at it. It would take a lot of finesse to get the drop on two people, especially if one of them was a cop. Even a crappy one." Mitch paused and cleared her throat. Her voice sounded raw. Was she crying?

"I know." I didn't want to hear what had happened next. But I had to. I'd seen the way the bodies were positioned. I had an idea of how things had gone down. My hands were clammy, and the phone slipped a little in my hand as I strained to hear Mitch on the other end.

"He shot them both in the knees, and then he would've gone to Del first. He'd have been reeling and heading into shock. The killer would have had no problem drugging him into submission while keeping him awake to watch."

I nodded. My face iced over and the walls undulated like late-morning coastal waves. "Must've taken a heckuva lotta force to bludgeon a man and a woman to death with a sledgehammer."

The walls were shifting toward me. The roof of my mouth was sandpaper, tearing up my tongue.

"Or a heckuva lotta anger." Mitch sniffled.

"Lotta angry men out there." I threw it out as a shield.

"And a few angry women too." Mitch held the phone back up to her face. She wore a concerned expression, but her voice was cold hard steel.

"Now all we gotta do is find the right one."

CHAPTER TWELVE

Friday, March 25

I stomped through my bedroom, opening and closing drawers—pulling out jeans and a sweatshirt. I threw on the clothes and headed downstairs. In my mind, the fireplace glowed with a fury, and I couldn't look at it. The specter of what I'd just seen via Mitch's cell phone hung before me as I made myself a strong pot of French pressed coffee.

What were the rest of the guys saying about me this morning? Aware of its morbid power, I'd never given gossip any air to breathe. Who were they drawing into the pit of disbelief as every lie was cast about?

I poured my coffee, black, and sat down at the counter. My cell phone buzzed, confirming an appointment with Kira Stoklavich, the department's therapist, at eight this morning. Maybe she could help me sort fact from fiction.

You shall know the truth, and the truth shall set you free.

Whoa! Where had that come from? And how the heck was I gonna find the truth? How big a life of its own had the idea of me being a murderer taken on? I sipped the hot brew. My Magnificent Being and I could handle it. His glorious peace wrapped around me like a prayer shawl and freed my mind to wander. I finished my coffee, picked up my gym bag, and paused to grab my barn coat. Just touching it brought back pleasant memories.

Gray legs, replete with sculpted muscles, pounding down the rail … poetry in motion as his graceful silhouette floated down the arena fence. A great big, beautiful, 17.2 hand quarter horse gelding named Scooter waited for me across town. *I gotta go see a woman about a horse.*

A quick barn visit would be just the elixir I'd need after my meeting with Kira. With any luck at all, I'd still be able to keep my coveted Friday visit with Samantha. Until my innocence was firmly established at the station, I had to tread carefully where Samantha was concerned.

During the past several weeks, I'd been hard at work gathering references, arranging home visits and interviews, and working through the legions of paperwork for the process of formally adopting my little girl. I was grateful beyond belief to have the afternoon with her to look forward to, but in light of the murder investigation, was it wise? As much as I wanted to see her, I didn't want to bring any more disruption into her life.

Maybe a better woman would wait until things calmed down. But I *needed* to see her. I prayed her little-girl warmth would envelope me like a cocoon and help me forget about the horror of the past thirty-six hours.

Other than Scooter, Samantha, and my mother, no one was really dying to see me. Funny what being the prime suspect in a gruesome double-murder case does to your calendar. Heat rushed to my face as the image of Cliff and Georgi, two of my dearest friends, passed quickly through my mind. *I'll call them next.*

I tossed my gym bag in the back seat and settled into my squad car. It felt good to be at the wheel again. Before backing down the driveway, I voice-dialed my mother's number and left a message telling her I'd be stopping by soon. My phone chirped, and I turned it over. The screen lit up with Donna's face, and I smiled into the cold plastic. "Hey."

"That's not the most articulate greeting you've ever offered me. But far from the worst. Do you want me to call Georgi for you, or have you already talked to her?"

I sighed. "Yes. Please." How I ever got so lucky to have such amazing friends was beyond me. *Thank you, God.*

"You know she can stay with me."

Donna had probably already invited her.

I lifted my eyes to the sky. "I'm so grateful for you both. Yes. Call her. Have her bring all the cheese and chocolate she can carry. We're in for a few long days. And I need you both by my side. I'm off to see Dr. Stoklavich."

"By yourself?" She raised her voice.

"Yes." I swallowed.

"Are you really okay going to this appointment alone, sweetie?" Her voice carried me into a safety zone. She and her husband Jim had been my saviors many a night. That they lived next door was one of the Seven Wonders of the World to me. In fact, their house disappeared from my rear-view mirror as I headed out of the subdivision.

"I'm not comfortable with your professional obligations with Kira. I still haven't forgiven her for how she treated you during your last visit. And I just don't like the woman." Donna's nerves had not been soothed when I explained the reason for my visit. Kira had never been my staunchest supporter. Water under the bridge.

"Thank you. But c'mon, it's not going to be that bad. Sure, Kira's an odd and elegant duck. She'll be decked out in some designer's fantasy, staring at me with that bemused look on her face while I serve my time on her leather sofa." I attempted a giggle and failed.

"And tell me again why you have to see that hateful woman." Donna's tone underscored her distaste.

"It's simple. Caring for my mental health makes me look even better as a prospective parent, especially in my line of work. And getting back to my normal activities might help everyone around me relax a little and stop focusing on the double murder. The sooner people start seeing me again instead of the all the chaos around me, the sooner I get to continue the adoption process in earnest."

"And finally become Samantha's forever family." Warmth radiated from her voice.

"Yes. At least I *think* that's my heart's desire." My lip quivered.

Did I just say those words out loud? Samantha's little body pressed up tight against mine in one of her welcome bear hugs swept through my mind, and a small smile erupted from my heart. But then a wave of fear slammed against me. I managed to keep talking. Letting the secret out had broken the dam of self-doubt.

"What if I'm no good at it? What if she gets sick? What if, four days into this, she hates me, and I'm a failure as a mother? Then where will she go? What if I fail at being a wife *and* a mom?" I was wandering through the city streets, palms pounding the wheel to emphasize my fears. "What if I can't keep her safe?"

"You've got to calm down. I wish you could see yourself the way Jim and I see you. You're strong, resilient, kind, and supremely capable. You'll make a wonderful mother. You two belong together. I just know it."

"Can I borrow some of that confidence?" I balanced my cell phone between my neck and my ear as I drove. "And thank you for listening to me and not judging me. It's like an eighteen-wheeler's been lifted off my chest."

"You're not much of an actress, you know. Live next door to someone for ten years, and you pick up on a few things. I could smell your fear from my house. You got this one, Jo. You really do. You're going to be an amazing mom. Now suck it up and go see that frightful woman. *Ciao*."

She hung up before I could thank her again. The silence in the wake of my confession stirred up more troubling questions. My anxious thoughts kept me grounded all the way to Kira's office.

CHAPTER THIRTEEN

Friday, March 25

The Paradise County courthouse had been designed during the turn of the previous century, with corrections in mind—thick, stone walls and all. I'd often wondered if violence broke out in a courtroom whether or not the guards posted right outside would be able to hear it and respond in time. Just another happy-snappy passing thought accompanying me through the security stations.

I kept my head down during my musings, all the way up the stone staircase and into the reception area of the Mental Health Services office. A blast of heat shot out from the open door behind the empty receptionist's desk. Kira stood in the doorway in a stylish suit, smiling at me like a wolf tracking a rabbit in a snowstorm.

"Good morning, Chief. Are you ready to rumble?" She tilted her head toward her office and winked.

Her eyes weren't smiling. I shivered and walked past her into her office, settling myself onto the soft, leather sofa. I pulled my arms out of my wool coat, leaving it cocooned around me like a shield. I closed my eyes to calm myself, offering silent prayers that this time would be worthwhile, asking God to help me think of topics that would make it clear I was trying hard to cooperate.

It wasn't the cop thing that had me sweating. Managing cops and criminals was second nature to me. The thought of parenting full time, and on my own, terrified me. Being with Samantha, taking care of her, being there for her—that was easy and filled my heart with peace and the deepest love I'd ever known. Thinking of myself as her mother—as anyone's mother—kept me up at night.

What if I fail? What if I'm a horrible mother? What if I have to work and can't find a sitter? What if Donna can't come through in a pinch? What if there's no room at the local day care the day I really need emergency assistance? What if? What if? What if?

"Are you, Josie?" Kira's voice had taken on the cool edge she got upon repeating herself.

What had she just asked me? Had I said anything so far? I had to get with the program if I ever wanted to have a shot at finding out if I had what it took to be a mom. So I decided to go on the offensive and just dive right in.

"Hey, you should be proud of me. I already know the issues I want to discuss today. There are a few, and I'm ready to unpack them all with you." *That* had to be worth some major shrink points. Due to reading back issues of my favorite magazine, I felt like I was getting the lingo down pat.

"Oh, really? Do tell. Pick one, and let's begin." She wasn't buying it. Clever of her to throw the ball back in my court, though.

"Okay, let's go for the mother lode, then."

"And what exactly might that be?" Her voice was smooth river stone while her lips shifted back toward an insincere smile.

"Ah, well, that's it—the mother lode of motherhood." I sat back, sighing like a flattening tire. Three minutes into the session, and I was already sharing real things. That wasn't in the plan.

"So, what are you feeling about this?" Her eyes bored into mine like a bare light bulb in a dark basement.

Did she think I was lying to her? Did she think I was hiding something? *Was* I hiding something?

"Nothing. Well, everything. It's just that I so very much want to adopt Samantha, and I'm scared to death at the same time and embarrassed to be struggling with these strong feelings. But I can't seem to shake them. I mean I'm happy and everything, and I really want to be her mom. But what if I fail her? I've never been a mom before. Everyone seems to do it with relative ease, like they know something I don't."

Tears moistened my eyes, and my chest tightened. I hated to confess my fears, show my weakness, to a woman I trusted so little. And who held the pen to my future. For a hundred and ten bucks an hour.

Maybe I could pretend I was talking to Donna, and I was here to really let 'er rip. What harm could it do to share some real fear and see what happened? I'm safe here, right? Then why did I feel like I had an open wound in the middle of an ocean filled with sharks? *Calm down, shut up, and talk.*

I decided to stick a toe in, start with the feelings. Kira'd like that whole feelings thing. "I like the way she feels lying next to me on the sofa when I visit her at the Murrays."

"Go on." She didn't seem all that thrilled with my opener.

"She feels like a puppy lying there sometimes. Like she has all the faith in the universe that I'll protect her and take care of her. She just closes her eyes and relaxes into me without a care in the world. I love that feeling. And I'm afraid I'm not worthy of it."

"Where does that fear come from?" Kira sat up straight, grabbing her computer tablet's stylus.

I stared at her, trying to guess what she was after. Nothing came to me after rolling her question around in my mind.

"You fear not being worthy of Samantha's trust. Why? What happened to make you feel unworthy?"

"Umm, I'm not sure." I was hoping I could hold out until the end of the session, get her to go off on one of her tangents. If I knew one thing about Kira, it was that she loved to hear herself talk. Whereas I hated giving voice to my doubts. Was I cut out for this? What would happen if I hated being a mother six months after finalizing the adoption? An oppressive cloud descended, and my thoughts swam through a sea of darkness. I shook it off, making a mental note to reward myself with a trip to the gourmet popcorn store on the way home.

"You've talked about this feeling of something not being right about *your* parents. How old were you when you realized your parents were different? That something about them was missing?" Kira was acting like a real therapist today. I might get my money's worth, for once.

"Uh, I don't know. Maybe six or seven?"

"And how old is Samantha?"

"Right now?" I was stalling—trying to figure out where she was going.

"Yes, right now." Kira sighed and half-rolled her eyes.

Can therapists do that? Kind of obnoxious, but then again, this is Kira.

"Almost seven." The light snapped on in my head. "Whoa. That's pretty good, doc. So what's it mean? What am I afraid of?"

"That's a great question. It sounds a little bit like abandonment to me. How does that sit with you? Are you maybe afraid you'll abandon Samantha like your parents abandoned you? That would be hard to face." She was saying semi-compassionate things, but her tone was flat.

"No! No way. I would never leave her, but I do think about whether or not I'm good enough for her. Whether or not I'm cut out to be a mother." Steel bands wrapped around my ribcage, and my throat constricted.

"No one is ever ready to be a parent. Kids just happen when they happen. That should be a bumper sticker: 'Parenting happens.' And people survive it." She smiled, satisfied with her quip, and glanced at her watch as she sat back in her chair.

"But not everybody does, right? Survive?" If I tossed a few questions at her, she might keep yapping and save me the trouble. Maybe get me through the last twenty-odd minutes of today's session.

"Well, now, that depends. Doesn't it? And not everyone *deserves* to survive, wouldn't you agree?" She slithered back slightly, nestling deeper into her chair, her hose rubbing against the upholstery.

"Sounds like we're no longer talking about parenting. Where'd we wander? Who doesn't deserve to survive?" Was she talking about Del? Images of my ex and his girlfriend bleeding to death on the boathouse floor wavered through my mind like a funhouse mirror. She couldn't be suggesting that Del deserved to die, could she?

"We're here to talk about anything you want. Several times since the Mentor Sister Killer was apprehended, you've introduced the notion that the kinds of people who would actively harm a defenseless child, like Samantha, shouldn't be allowed to live. I believe you said something akin to 'they don't deserve to survive.' Tell me more about that." She took a few notes without looking down at her computer tablet as she talked, holding my gaze.

Had I said that? I didn't think so. I'd certainly thought that. And I'd had the occasional fantasy about rounding up the bad guys and putting them in the ground. Maybe I did say it. Lord knows my mind wanders in these sessions. Might as well go with it.

"Yeah, there are lots of perps who deserve to die. Lots of them. So what?"

"So, what I'm wondering is how you feel about living in a world where people can do bad things to good people and get away with it. Does the lack of justice bother you?" She'd taken on a sonorous tone, like a judge.

"Of course it ticks me off. I'd love to get my gun and put those punks in the ground—make this world a safer place for everyone." *You're an idiot! You're under investigation for murder and you start talking like this? Do you want to get back to work or not?* I closed my eyes, focused on relaxing my shoulders, softening my belly. "But I'll settle for putting them behind bars. Wrap my arms tight around all the Samanthas on the planet, and make sure nobody else can harm them. But—"

"But what? You don't have the power? Or you don't *take* the power?" Sonorous shifted to sharp.

"I don't have that kind of power. I don't *want* that kind of power. That's not my job while here on this Earth. That's God's job. I'm not the judge and jury, and I don't aspire to be."

"You may not *be* the judge and jury, as you say, but are you *sure* you don't want to be? Don't you get a deep sense of satisfaction every time—and I quote—'one of those evil perps gets what's coming to them?'" She referred to her notes as she spoke.

I'd ranted on this topic more than once. I didn't remember using those words exactly. It sounded like something I *could've* said though.

"Alright. Yeah, sure. Who doesn't want to see creeps like the Mentor Sister Serial Killer punished?" I squirmed deep into the old cushions. Who wouldn't want to see him fry rather than know he's taking up space in a federal prison waiting on the legal system to decide his fate? He killed nine women that we knew of—probably more. What kind of justice is there, in a case like that? Talking about the man who'd kidnapped Samantha in a desperate attempt to lure me into a death trap sucked me into a dark vortex.

Nature abhors a vacuum; Kira jumped in.

"As you once said, 'an eye for an eye and a tooth for a tooth.' Death should be justice enough. I remember you telling me, how did you put it, that some men were meant to be captured and killed?" She looked up from her notes, face flushed, tiny beads of sweat marring her forehead. "Don't you worry about a thing, Chief. Your secrets are safe with me."

Then why don't I feel safe with her? I pulled myself to my feet, grabbed my coat, and turned to face her one last time before leaving her office.

"Thanks," I muttered, averting my eyes on my way out the door.

CHAPTER FOURTEEN

Friday, March 25

I soldiered through the hallways without interacting with anyone. Head down, dark clouds of oppression thundering through my mind, I crashed through the last set of doors, desperate for fresh air. I leaned up against the courthouse wall and pulled out my phone, thumbed through pictures of Sam like a starving woman, smiled, and pushed off the wall. Walking into the sunlight cheered my spirit. My revived mindset gave me a great idea. I brightened further as I punched in Gino's number while I clipped through the parking lot.

"M'hija! You *do* remember me!" Laughter barreled through the speaker of my car's Bluetooth. I pulled out of the parking lot on autopilot.

"You know where I'm headed, right?" I drew out the last word.

"Ah, she thinks how clever she is. Well, perhaps she would like to know that I am already there. Right?" He drew out the last word too, teasing me back.

"Oh, really? Me, too." Traffic was light. We'd be giving our usual breakfast order somewhere between the morning and noon crowds today. Perfect.

"And your penchant for less than complete honesty has earned you the right to buy my breakfast this day. *Pero*, I will buy. This time." His end of the line went silent, leaving me to fend for myself as I wove through traffic, hit the parking lot, and followed the incredible aromas into our favorite breakfast haunt.

It took all of two seconds to spy his handsome face, broad shoulders, and chambray-clad boxer's body crammed into a 50s-style vinyl booth. He raised an eyebrow and waved me over. When I was two strides from the booth, he rose and stepped forward to fold me into his arms. We didn't speak as we hugged, happy and at peace in each other's company.

"Sit, and tell me all about your time with *La Mala*." Gino had never been a fan of Kira. His Cuban roots meant he valued healers over therapists and Catholics over practicing atheists. He'd created an elite company in the world of security and prisoner transportation, depending upon brute strength, firepower, and high-tech gadgets alike to get his point across. There wasn't a whole lot of room in his world for stifling regulations like having to be cleared by a cop shrink to get back to work after doing your job. Gino was old school.

"What'll it be, handsome?" A curvy waitress appeared at our booth, smacking her gum for emphasis.

"I would like scrambled egg whites with a pinch of salsa on the multigrain toast, *por favor*." Gino smiled up at her, grabbed my menu and handed them both to her. "And she will have the same."

"What? No, I'll take the breakfast hash with two eggs, over easy, and all the fresh coffee you've got." I kicked his foot under the table as she walked off. "Hey, *handsome*. In the future, leave my meal planning to me."

I doctored up the mug of coffee when it arrived and sampled it. Not bad.

"Enough of these coquetries. You must now tell me all that happened in the office of La Mala today." Gino rolled his head from side to side— one of his least endearing habits. He was always moving some body part around in some unnatural direction, like a workout-to-go.

"Where do I begin?"

Ugh. Today's session. But talking to Gino was more therapeutic than talking to Kira. I'd bored Gino to heck and back with the depth of my grief. Ever since I learned about Del's affair, through the winding trail of my near-divorce, to the reality of what had happened during the past forty-eight hours, Gino'd been one of my closest confidants. And he'd never complained once. I didn't deserve this man, but I was forever grateful he was in my life.

"I want to hear it all, m'hija. Anytime, anyplace."

"I think I'm just going to start collecting cats or something." The waitress appeared midsentence. We took a break from talking for a few minutes as we tucked into our respective meals.

"Now, having finished a light breakfast, and seeing that you are finished shoving those carbs into your mouth. Let us take advantage of this moment. I know you must be struggling. But now you are beset with the demons of 'what if' and the tricks of the mind that create false memories. And you are surviving even that. But what I do not know is *how*. How do you survive those dark moments, m'hija?" He leaned forward, broad brown face so close our foreheads almost touched.

This dear man had been so patient with me. If anyone had earned a glimpse into the torture that was my soul, it was Gino.

"I keep going, G. I keep on walking, and I don't look back. At least, not with my head." I drummed my fingers on the ancient Formica tabletop long enough for Gino to take my hand in his and squeeze.

"But your heart has been another story. Your heart was broken into a thousand pieces the day we learned of the great betrayal. And now, with what has just happened, I am worried for you and your hurting heart." He let my hand go and wiped at an invisible tear.

I blinked back a tear of my own. "I wish I could say I was devastated. But all I am is numb. I thought it'd be easier, you know? Getting over my wreck of a marriage? Yet several months later, I think I'm still in love with a man in love with somebody else—both of whom just happen to be dead." I picked up a saltshaker and studied it, waiting for my hands to steady before continuing. "How hopeless am I? I keep trying to think past it—past *them*. Sometimes the fantasy slinks back in."

My shoulders hunched, and my head dropped toward my chest.

"What kind of fantasy could you still hold in your heart for a man of his kind? One who treated you so badly, who hurt you so deeply. I am not sorry to say I do not regret his death." Gino's soft brown eyes glistened. "Even on Good Friday, a day that reminds me of forgiveness, sacrifice, and new life, even today, I struggle with my anger over this man. That is my struggle. How I wish I could lift it from your shoulders."

"It's not that simple. Not that clean. He's … he's *everywhere*. There isn't a place in my life unmarked by him—by images of us. I loved throwing parties together. I loved seeing the pride on his face as he showed me off in the beginning, the comfort of knowing he'd always be there for me. In public, anyway." A wistful tone crept into my voice.

"But that which was happening in private was much less happy, *verdad*?" Compassion flowed from him, and he wrapped his fingers around mine. "M'hija, don't allow the warmth of these memories to distort the clarity of the not-so-good ones. What about your memories of his drinking? Or his lies? Or the constant disappointment seasoning your very life as he broke one promise after another? Do you not remember this as well?"

"That part I *don't* miss—him telling me he was working late while I was sitting in the nearly empty parking lot of the station, soaking up the lie." I squeezed his hand, knocking my calves together under the table.

"You called me from that very lot that night. That man was a devil and a fool." He clasped my hand, turned it palm up.

"All the times I confronted him … his cool derision when caught in one of his way too many lies. The sound of his voice leaving me a thousand messages—his belligerent tone defending his heartless actions time after time. You win, Gino. Lord knows I don't miss that." I grimaced at my mountain-sized friend.

"Nobody wins in this case—not even the dead. *Favor* m'hija, you must not permit him to tear you apart from the grave. He did enough damage when he was alive. Allow the dead to stay dead, and let us learn to live *con gusto*. There is more. *Te prometo que haya mas*." He pulled out his trucker's wallet and placed two folded twenties beside his plate, another over–the-top tip, Gino-style.

We slid out of the booth in unison. He drew me into his arms before leaving me standing outside. I watched him walk away, wondering about his promise. Was there really more for me?

The truth of who Del was, the reality of us, who I had become over time in order to please him and find a sad contentment with him … my freedom was a gift. But the solitude and loneliness that came with freedom sucked. I was accustomed to having a man by my side. In my house. In my bed. In my life.

But the freedom was worth the pain.

Wasn't it?

CHAPTER FIFTEEN

Friday, March 25

My impromptu breakfast with Gino had edged out my barn time. Samantha and I had a visit scheduled for today that included lunch, and I didn't want to miss a second with her. I scrolled through my contacts and called her social worker, William Greene. He was the reason I'd made it through the foster parent training program without bailing. He spotted my fear before I did—and was still helping me every time it cropped up by reminding me that no one's prepared for parenthood—until they step into it.

He answered in his soulful way. "Peace. What's up?"

"My girl, that's what." The thrill of a fast gallop on a cold morning flew through my belly.

He was silent.

"Today's my day. Our day. I'm on my way." I leaned over the steering wheel, closer to the Bluetooth microphone for emphasis.

"Ah, Jo, I heard about your—about Del. I'm sorry." His voice was too quiet.

"Thank you." Formality crept into my tone.

"I'm guessing you haven't received the court order forbidding you to visit her for the time being. I've heard some chatter on the matter. What I haven't heard is a definitive answer."

He knew I'd been a suspect. *Am I still a suspect?*

"That's been cleared up." That wasn't true. I'd asked the amazing trio not to share my whereabouts beyond the three of them for as long as possible. They must've honored my request. *Crap.*

"I'm sure it has. Still, let's wait a while on scheduling a visit, get a little distance between these murders and our girl. Give the system time to push the information through the proper channels." There was a firmness in his voice that would be too much work to fight.

"Fine. Tell her I love her, okay? Tell her something came up, but I'll see her in a couple a days. Thanks, pal." I ended the call without waiting to hear anything else. It wasn't his fault, but he was handy.

I pulled into a gas station parking lot to regroup. Should I go ride Scooter in my newly freed up time? I called Mitch and asked her to set up a briefing on the murder with me and the two lead FBI agents in a few hours. The beauty of a small town cop shop. They needed all hands on deck, mine included.

"Ah, Chief, you sure that's a good idea?" Mitch wasn't about to come any closer to the dynamite hanging in the air between us.

"Yes. A hundred percent. Any minute now, one or both of us will get the call that clears me to the proverbial 'T.'" *I hope.*

"Sure, but ..."

"And when it does, why waste time pulling you together?" Prickly heat inched up under my chin.

"Well, even when you're cleared, and even in an understaffed, overworked little burg like Haversport, it might not be the best thing to have you working this case though, right?"

Only Mitch had earned the right to speak this kind of truth to me.

"So, you think there's a better cop than me to work this case?" It was a stupid thing to say. My shirt was sticking to my back, my social worker wouldn't let me see my little girl, my cheating ex was dead, and I was about to get a whole lot stupider.

"Josie ..." Mitch sighed.

"I'm sorry. You're the cop to work this case, and we have a dozen others. But I can't stay out of this one. I don't care what the ruling is. I can't. I won't." I gripped the steering wheel with both hands, watching my veins plump up.

"I get it. And I'm all for you putting in an appearance as more of a Chief, less of a suspect. But only if it's going to help you, not hurt you, in the long run."

I sighed. "I appreciate you and your concern. I do. Set up the meeting so we're good to go the minute we get the call." My voice was crisper than I'd meant it to be. "Thanks, Mitch."

I hung up before she could reply and headed to the outskirts of town. Instead of riding my horse, I would stop by Riverside and visit my mother while waiting for the phone to ring.

CHAPTER SIXTEEN

Friday, March 25

Riverside Place was built ten years ago as an "independent living center for active seniors" in unincorporated Haversport. The town had grown up enough to almost touch the property, but Riverside still had that 'towne country feeling' boasted about in its literature. Bluffs jutted up in the distance on three sides of the facility, giving the seniors excellent views from most balconies and patios. My mom had called this place home for the past four years.

I parked in my usual spot and signed the guest register. A dull roar floating down the hallway on the right reminded me it was Friday Happy Hour. Oh, brother—I didn't have it in me today to watch wheelchair-bound ninety-year-old studs flirt with half a dozen adoring fellow residents. Seemed like everyone had a partner—except for me.

Shake it off, sister! I pushed through my melancholy and pulled myself down the hall. Dick Clark was up on a big screen, and there were streamers everywhere. Who knew what holiday was being commemorated here today. Certainly not Good Friday. It didn't matter. Silver heads bobbed with simple glee, and I stopped to greet my mother's friends and neighbors as I kept an eye out for her.

A cane tapped the back of my leg. I turned to face a dignified gentleman, with sparkling blue eyes, in a wheelchair. "Chief! Have one on me."

Art Spenser held out a plastic cup of something questionable.

I took the offering from his shaking hand and bent down to kiss his cheek. "Thanks, Art. How are you? You're looking great."

His fingers circled my wrist with practiced ease. "Your mother needs you. She don't look so good." His crepe paper voice crinkled with worry. "Look in on her?"

"You know she hates these things. Though if you're here, she usually is too." *Was she sick? Why hadn't the staff brought her? Having another bad day?*

"Look in on her." He squeezed my wrist and then let it go.

"Thanks. I'm on my way. Go easy on the ladies." I winked at him and gave him a quick one-armed hug.

Clipping down the hall away from the excitement, my phone vibrated. I turned right and headed into the assisted living wing, tugging my phone out of my pocket. Frank McKinley, Paradise County Sheriff. This was the news I'd been waiting for. It had to be.

"Mac. Thanks for calling." I threw the words out without thinking. "What do you know?"

"Afternoon, Josie. I hope you're well. You know I want what's best for you." Mac's deep voice poured over me. Good news? Bad news?

"I know that." I quieted my tone, tried to calm myself. Mac could not be rushed.

"I know you're going to want to work a case we both know you should not be working. I know I'd be wanting to do the exact same thing. I'm not going to tell you you can work this case. I'm just going to tell you that you've been cleared to return to work by Dr. Stoklavich."

I sucked in a deep breath, raised my head to the ceiling, slow-counted to ten, released it. "Oh, thank God."

"Yes, thank God as I'm sure He's got a hand in this, and I'm even surer that He'd want His best working the case." Mac's message was clear—even if he didn't want to say it out loud. You never knew who could be listening in on conversations at the courthouse. "And you are the best, Chief Oliver. Just be wise about it. And lean on your right hand man." He ended the call before I could squeak out my appreciation.

I sent Mitch a quick text telling her I was cleared and back in the game while heading to my mother's room. Just as I reached her door, Mitch responded.

Showtime in thirty minutes. Never doubted you. ☺

I tapped on the door as I pushed it open. The hum and whoosh of the oxygen machine greeted me. My mother was not in her little living room. I followed the oxygen hose to her bedroom and tip-toed inside. She was asleep, a peaceful smile lending her face a sweetness in the wan light. Her little bird's body was swathed in a mound of home-spun blankets. I slipped to the side of the bed, touched her arm and bowed my head.

Dear God, thank you so much for my mother. Watch over her and please heal her from any physical issues she might be struggling with today. Please give her a strong sense of Your presence deep in her heart, in her spirit, even as she sleeps. I love you, Mighty God. Thank You.

After watching her sleep and praying a moment longer, I left Riverside, going as fast as my municipal plates could take me.

I pulled the squad car into the empty space next to Mitch's cruiser near the front door of the station. From the looks of the parking lot, she'd gathered the A Team to greet me. I offered a silent prayer of thanks for this show of respect. Of course, it could also be the first subtle sign of impending mutiny. *Hope for respect and be ready to settle for simple acquiescence.*

My hands gripped the cool leather of the steering wheel hard enough to send tremors through my arms all the way up to my shoulders. I sat still for several seconds, peering into the tinted glass doorway, as if I had the power to divine what may or may not be happening on the other side of the vestibule.

The door pushed open and a diminutive blonde materialized in the bright sunlight. Even in a drab navy shirtdress, the woman commanded attention. Her cornflower blue eyes smiled as our glances met, and I climbed out of my car. She waited for me to join her on the landing.

"Liz! Girl, you are a sight for sore eyes! What in the world are you doing out here? Waiting for me to arrive so you can give me a police escort?" As soon as the words flew out of my mouth, her darkening eyes confirmed it. My smile froze, and my throat went ice cold.

Something was wrong. Very, very wrong.

CHAPTER SEVENTEEN

Friday, March 25

Liz stood before me, clasping and unclasping her hands. I took a deep breath and squeezed her trembling forearm. It dropped to her side.

"It's okay, Liz. Whatever it is, we'll handle it. What's going on?"

"There's been another murder."

My head whipped back. Electricity jolted through me.

"A murder? Where? When? Who was the victim? And why are you out here telling me this on the station stairs? Why are we not inside with the boys sifting through the details?" My shoulders stiffened.

"It's not just that." Her eyes dropped to the concrete.

"Go on."

"The guys have been wondering out loud about you. About your absence. About the, well, the other thing …"

"And what else have they been wondering about?" My temples throbbed.

"About whether or not your fitness routine includes any sledgehammering." Her eyes darted from the sidewalk to just over my right shoulder as she spoke.

"The victim was murdered with a … sledgehammer?" I leaned against the railing, uttering the last word in a whisper. "Who was the vic, Liz?" The cold steel soothed my lower back.

"The victim was also a perp. And honestly, to hear Mitch tell it, half the guys don't even care who did it, and the other half want to track the killer down and give him—or her—a community service award."

"He was that bad?" The muscles in my face relaxed, and a gentle warmth washed over me.

"Yes, he really was that bad. And you know him."

"*I* know him?" My brain wandered through a thick, black forest, as numbness seeped into me. What was she trying to say, without telling me?

"You've arrested him on three different occasions. The last one was pretty recent. A few days before the, uh, the other thing."

I smiled at Liz's inability to refer directly to the murder of Del and his girlfriend.

But then I frowned. "Deter? Did somebody off Deter?" I pulled my head back, brows arched.

"Yes. The victim is—was—Derrick Deter." She looked me straight in the eye. There wasn't a hint of a smile there.

"Somebody killed Deter with a *sledgehammer*?" My first second back on the job, and my professional life just took a major turn off course.

"Yes. But that's not all."

"That's not enough?" I snorted. The news of Deter's demise was transforming me back into my scrappy self in a hurry. Things could not be any worse than this. Which was sort of like saying they'd get better—right?

"It's more than enough. But it's not all. He was shot in the kneecap, drugged, and *then* beaten to death with a sledgehammer."

CHAPTER EIGHTEEN

Friday, March 25

The weight of Liz's worry pulled at my shoulders as we treaded the station hallway. Dark murmurings slipped from the bullpen around the corner. Half a dozen detectives circled the white board. Coffee cups littered desktops.

Mitch was holding court.

She plucked an unlit cigarette out of Garret's mouth and stomped on it midsentence, just as the sound of Liz's footsteps walking toward our offices announced my presence in the back of the room. All heads turned. Cold, hard stares interspersed with the occasional nod welcomed me back.

I looked around the room, ready to butt heads. One guy in particular would push me to the mat today. Walt Schlichting, an angry, woman-hating cop who just happened to land on my force against my will. But that's the way the cookie crumbles when a public board makes your department's personnel decisions. And guess who had an uncle serving on that board? *He's missing. Good.*

I walked up to Mitch. She held the dry erase marker out to me and joined the guys. Should I have taken it from her? Maybe I should have just kept walking back to my office. The lines were blurred for all of us. Tension rushed through the room like a California wildfire.

"Garret was just about to brief the team, Chief." Mitch's eyes were trained on the wall behind me.

I nodded to Noah Garret, a newly-assigned detective. He'd put in for a transfer to our department about a year ago. Word on the street was he was running from some marital drama of his own. Mitch nudged him, and he started to talk.

"I was just saying that the murder has the same MO as the, the uh …" His voice trailed off, and he looked at my feet.

Forget it. I'm staying put. I will not be run out of my own bullpen.

"The gruesome murder of my husband and his girlfriend?" My voice was a slab of steel.

I would claim the respect of my guys during this murder investigation. Even if it killed me. Nausea threatened to overwhelm me. The tortured souls that were Del and his girlfriend swirled around my brain.

"Yes." He drew his gaze from my feet to my eyes.

"Well, go on, detective. Continue." I gave him the dry erase marker and sat on the corner of the desk closest to the whiteboard.

Garret straightened his shoulders and spoke again. "Derrick Deter. White male, forty-five years old. His jacket is, was, a mile long. None of the fun stuff, either. He was a first-class perp. Arrested for suspected child molestation in four states. Did some time in Nevada. Made his way to the land of Lincoln and set up shop about eight and a half years ago. Got a job as a school custodian. Under a different name."

Mitch slipped a fat folder into my hands. Deter's arrest photos stuck to the inside cover. A summary of his arrests and behavior during his numerous overnights with us told the story of a man who danced around the flames of justice without ever getting burned. Garret's voice droned on as I skimmed the monster's history.

We all knew this story. Most of the detectives around the board had worked on a case involving Deter during the past several years. None of them had been able to gather enough evidence to book him, though. Not even me. I knew it in my bones—he was guilty of everything we suspected him of and more. Probably much more. I was glad he was dead. And I kind of liked that he suffered in the end.

What kind of a monster did that make *me*?

"So, whadda we got?" I stood and faced my hostile team. No one spoke. Eyes flitted about in search of a safe place to land. Mitch was still looking slightly past me. I stared at her, shifting my body to coax her into an involuntary glance back at me. It worked.

"So, the MO matches." She lifted her eyes back over my shoulder. Just enough to look like she was respecting me publicly without aligning with me privately. Trying to tell me with her actions what she couldn't tell me with her words?

Does she think I should stand down from this investigation?

"What, are you a minimalist now?" I cocked my eyebrow and slanted my head in her direction.

A few of the guys snickered. Mitch didn't answer. I waited. Three seconds. No one spoke. Five seconds. She leaned back and crossed her arms. Ten seconds. I stared at her until she met my gaze. Fifteen seconds.

"Yup. Welcome back, Chief." She gave me the barest hint of a nod and uncrossed her arms.

"Thanks, Mitch. And thanks to all of you for carrying on in light of all the craziness surrounding me right now. It's good to be back. Now let's go catch this creep before he kills again. Garret, pull up what we know so far about the unsub. Nano, get us what you've researched on similar crimes in the past ten years here and across the country. Let's get mapping, team. We're going to spend the next two hours going through every detail. At the end of our review, I want to see some solid leads on where this killer's going to strike next. We gotta get ahead of his game. *Now*."

Heads nodded and the guys broke off in clusters, murmuring together. Mitch was talking with two veteran detectives, her back to me. I stepped over to her and tapped her shoulder blade.

"Let's go." I turned and walked toward my office. Would she follow me?

"Bring it to me when you chase it down. I'll be with the Chief." Mitch's voice was clipped. Reluctant footsteps indicated she was with me, at least in body, if not in spirit. Liz's eyes widened as we passed her desk on our way to my office, single file, in silence.

"Would you like some—"

"Yes, Liz, coffee would be a real life saver. The usual. For both of us, please." My smile was for Liz alone. One more routine taken back in the fight to recapture my standing in my own station. I waited by the door as Mitch walked stiffly past me into my office, and then closed the door. She folded into one of the club chairs in front of my desk. I sat on the edge of my desk with my arms crossed, staring at her.

"Mitch, you gotta knock off this crap. I get it that your faith in me is maybe waning a little bit after spending time alone with the guys. Maybe it's getting harder for you to have my back in front of them when they don't know all the facts. But you gotta choose, girl. You can't have it both ways. You got my back, or not?"

Her face softened for a second. Then she disappeared into a brooding silence again. Her lips quivered in defiance. "I dunno, Chief. I don't like it."

"You don't like what?" My eyes narrowed to a squint.

"We've got three high-profile murders in as many days. That's more action than this village has ever seen. And, two of them were … Should you *really* be involved in this?" Her defiance melted into frustration.

"I know, Mitch. He was my husband. But I can't just sit this one out. Maybe I should. Maybe a better woman would. But I can't." My admission came out in a steady cadence.

She sucked in a belly full of air and let it out in a noisy gush. "I know, I know. I'm sorry. It's just that if this were my investigation …"

"But it isn't." I cut her off.

"Right. But if I were the Chief of Police, I might not necessarily think it wise for you to be leading the charge on this one." Her tone was apologetic, but her body remained tense. "I'm sorry, but that's the way I feel."

"Well, that's just great that we're sharing our feelings here. 'Cause I got some of my own to share." My voice sharpened with every word. "There's only one chief in this station, Mitch." I stood up and moved into her personal space, towering above her. "And you ain't it."

Dark red clouds moved across her face. Her hands, gripping the slender armrests, were turning white. I moved back two steps to lean on the desk again. The clouds lightened, and her shoulders lowered two inches, but she kept her eyes trained on the wall beyond me.

"You got a problem with that?" I folded my arms, keeping my voice strong and steady.

"Not yet." She shook her head without relaxing another muscle or meeting my gaze.

"Good." I wouldn't be fazed. "'Cause I need you. This place needs you. Heck, this whole village needs you. A heckuva lot more than you need it, that's for sure. All I ask is that you put your fear and doubt aside—at least until we get this guy. The rest is up to you."

"I can't promise you it'll be like it was before." Her voice was still and low.

"Mitch! What is up with you?" Tension rocketed through my body. I must've missed something. Something *big*.

She stared at me, neck reddening. Her right eyelid twitched, and she snapped out of the chair, rifling through her jacket pockets. She pulled out a manila envelope and slammed it on the desk beside me. "There. Now that we've cleared the air, what do you make of this? Here's a full copy of a little special delivery sitting on Liz's desk this morning."

"What the heck is this?" I picked up the envelope and pried it open with my fingernails. Two glossy black and white photos slid onto the desktop. Each of them was a photo of one of the crime scenes, possibly right after the victims had been attacked. Definitely post mortem. One look at the lifeless eyes told me that much. I stared at Del's face, masked in death. Tears sprang from my eyes, and my stomach lurched.

Mitch reached for the photos and turned them over. She pointed at the name of the town, watermarked onto the paper. "You're seeing this, right?"

The pictures had been printed on the crime photo paper issued only to us and paid for by the taxpayers of Haversport. The paper was a sacred commodity, and very few people had access.

"Yeah, so?" I crossed my arms.

"And you agree with me that these shots had to be taken at the scene, right?" She looked at me.

"Yeah. So, someone did their job, catalogued the crime scene. And …?" I stomped my foot down on the carpet. Picked up my foot, stomped it again. *Thank God for sensible shoes.*

"So that's the problem. We did have a tech—the same tech, in fact, responsible for recording evidence at both scenes." She folded her fingers, cracked her knuckles, unfolded them. "Only problem is, we checked. Neither of these photos were taken by him or anyone else in our department. They don't match the ones you took with your cell phone either."

Her acknowledging I'd been at Del's crime scene alone lit a dim light. Was that why she was mad at me? I'd put myself in harm's way once again? I scrunched my brows and looked at her. "But then …"

"Exactly. Who took these shots? And how did they get the paper? And why put them on Liz's desk? And how did they do that without being seen? While we're at it, who would've known your whereabouts today?" Mitch moved over to the club chair and sank back into it, folding her feet underneath, giving her the appearance of a delicate warrior.

"Why are you asking?" Wariness flowed through the air between us.

"How many people would have had clearance and access to evidence from both crime scenes?" She glanced at me, pulled out her phone, and pressed it on.

"The real question is, how many cops were present at both crime scenes?" I leaned over the chair behind her. The staff report we were after materialized on her tiny screen.

"Five, six maybe? Check this out." Curiosity softened her voice.

"Good grief. Take a closer look. Read it to me." I pushed myself away, preparing to hear what I was certain I'd just read. I slumped into my chair behind the desk.

"Garrett. You. Me. Schlichting. Two of the FBI guys, counting Nick." She was whispering as the gravity of it all sunk in. She waited in silence for me to say what we were both thinking.

"Six of us, all told. So, which one—"

The muscles in her face bunched up as she stared at the tiny screen. Had something new cropped up?

She looked up at me, and blinked. "Corey Richardson not only has a history of assaults, but he works as a lab tech at Mercy Hospital."

CHAPTER NINETEEN

Friday, March 25

Mitch rocked back on her heels, edging her body ever so slightly away from my desk. I swiveled in my chair, rattled by the loud squeak of the base. Her body stiffened as she inhaled several little breaths.

"Jumpy, huh?"

"Chief... there's more on Richardson. He's been charged with assault; the report summary says it was over his wife's alleged infidelity—with a cop. And, you want to take a stab at his hobby?" She took a step back. Two more and she'd knock into the mahogany credenza lining the wall.

I shrugged my shoulders. "I got nothin'."

"He's a world-class amateur weight lifter." She nodded, as if this pulled the package together with a bow on top.

"'Roid rage? You're saying Richardson what, found out about the affair, and waited until the night before the divorce was final to take them both out? Why wait? And what possible connection could he have to Deter?" I looked up at the ceiling. "But we can't just give up on our dirty cop theory, can we? Who else but one of us would have access to these photos?"

Mitch's stony face gave nothing away.

"It's a lot to take in, I know. But what else could it mean?" I kept my eyes trained on hers.

"What *does* it mean? Is this the killer, playing with us?" Suspicion lined her face and didn't look good on her.

"Well, these shots didn't take themselves. And they're, without a doubt, from the crime scenes, but they are for sure not our work. Not officially anyway." I looked her right in the eye and cocked a leg out.

She stared at me with wide eyes. "Which tells us, what—that one of us took them at the scene right after we murdered a few people, then came down to the station to print them on 5x7 glossy?" Color drained from her face. She looked down at her feet. A slight tremble rolled over her. "So, Garrett is known as somewhat of an amateur photography buff."

"So are you. But I'm not even going there. How hot is Schlichting for this kind of thing? You know he hates my guts. Ever since I had him written up for 'conduct unbecoming' back in the good old days." I sat on the edge of my desk.

"Before he even started working for you. Yeah. Fun. I was there, remember? But I don't know, I'm not feeling it. How could it be him? Or *any* of the rest us?" She had backed into the credenza, and stood like a newborn calf in front of it.

She always hated the way I used anything as a chair. How much did she want to straighten the chair in front of my desk? I pushed my own chair out further at an odd angle with my foot.

"Or any of the rest of us. We're going to set this aside for the time being instead of dancing around each other. I don't have the energy to get into a pointless cat fight—"

She snorted, interrupting me. "Maybe a little Mitch slapping would be more appropriate."

That was pretty good. She was lightening up.

She snapped her head back and forth once. "So, if it isn't you, and it isn't me, that leaves four possibilities: Garret, the federal agent, and Nick."

"You forgot about Schlichting. And it ain't Nick. I can practically guarantee you it ain't Nick." At least, I hoped I could.

She sighed. "*Practically* doesn't do us much good. We don't know what we don't know about Nick."

"What's *that* supposed to mean?" Pain stippled through my heart. Was she holding something back?

"I know you two have a history. I know you've been through a few wars together. When you worked homicide in Chicago, nobody could beat your solve rates. And I know there've been one or two Nick sightings in the past few weeks." She fidgeted, casting her gaze away from me, picking up a paperweight from my credenza, studying it.

"Yeah, so?" I grabbed a pen off my desk and started clicking the top with my thumb.

"He's been seen in the company of a particular brunette." Her eyes stuck like glue to the wall of windows beyond us.

"A certain slender, rich brunette?" My heavy heart deadened.

"Yes." Mitch drew her eyes away from the window, closer to me.

"More than once?" Rapid heartbeats pounded through my body. White noise rushed my ears.

"Yes." She straightened up and fidgeted with her phone again.

"So, she's maybe back in the picture, then." Exhaustion rolled through me.

"Yes." She was scrolling through some photos. Her nervous tell. She would scroll through pictures of herself with her husband. Reminders of her life beyond the job.

"But we don't know what that means." I looked within myself and found a thousand possibilities. Most impossibly bleak. One or two could be legit.

"Well, I know one thing—he can't be trusted. Not completely." She seemed to choose her words with the utmost care. She stopped on one of the pictures. Her husband's square jaw came into view under her thumb.

"Could mean anything. Could be purely professional." *Could be.*

"Watch your back, Jo." She shoved her phone back into her jacket pocket before straightening my office chairs, nodding at me, and leaving me alone.

A flash of pain pulsed through my temples. My stomach was full of sludge. I wanted to sink into my chair, but I was paralyzed.

Nick and Kira? *Again?*

CHAPTER TWENTY

Friday, March 25

Mitch's steps smacked down the hallway toward the bullpen. The quiet in my office was far too loud for comfort, but nowhere near enough to drown out the roaring in my head. Steel rods shot up from my stomach, jamming my throat. I fought against the memories. Distorted thoughts slammed around me like an iron tomb. *First Del, now Nick?*

Would I ever be compelling enough for anyone to stay by my side forever? Would I always be that woman—the one men walked away from? How could I be so easily replaced?

I dragged myself over to shut the door and locked it for good measure. A darkness grew around me. Every fiber of my body was hardening cement. My arms and legs buzzed as they grew heavier, leaving me so weighted down that the walk over to the leather sofa against the wall felt like trudging through quicksand. I plopped down hard.

Nothing mattered. All I craved was out. Of this mess. Maybe out of more. Or maybe a drink. Anything to fill the great nothingness I swam through every day since Del left me … twice. I was standing on the edge of a slippery cavern floor, hot lava from a lake of sulfur gurgling just off shore. I struggled in my darkness for a moment, and then warmth like a blanket eased around me. Silk-wrapped words rolled through my mind, gilding a path, leading me into the light.

"I will allure her, and bring her into the wilderness, and speak tenderly to her … And in that day, declares the LORD, you will call me 'My Husband'." Gino's pastor had been preaching out of a little book called Hosea lately—about God's intimate love for us. God used the prophet and his less-than-virtuous wife, Gomer, to demonstrate the depth of His love for us, for me, even when we're at our worst.

I closed my eyes and took a deep breath. *Lord, help me to see my life through Your eyes. Help me to look to You first, to take comfort in You. To remember that You love me more than any earthly husband ever could.*

Maybe I wasn't ready to return to work after all. Conflicting beliefs and images rolled around in my psyche. The scene I most regretted tumbled back to mind. My naïveté knew no bounds.

Ruefully, I remembered one of our last nights.

Del and I, in bed. Days before he left. Me, in his arms, wrapped up in the soft bliss of willful ignorance.

"Del?" I had turned my head to search for his eyes in the dark.

"Hmm?" He tightened his hold.

"I'm so glad we have each other." I nestled my head into his chest and relaxed.

"Mm-hm." He rested his chin on my head.

"I heard rough stories tonight—saw so many sad faces. Being here with you makes me feel sad for the many people going it alone. It's such a luxury to wake up in your arms, to know you're always here for me."

I tasted despair and relief at the same time as we lay there in the dark. His random tenderness confused me. Nights like that made me wonder if I'd made up the rest. The daily agonies and indignities faded, and I clung to the warmth offered, willing myself to believe it could last. This time.

"And I always will be." He kissed me on the head, and I fell asleep in his arms within minutes.

Less than a week later, he left me for another woman. How was I supposed to come back from that?

I slid off the sofa and sank to my knees, my head slumping onto my chest. *Why do you even try?* Dry eyes stared long moments into nothingness. Since my department-issued Glock was still in the station's safe, my personal, privately-owned handgun was in my shoulder harness. I pulled it out and placed it on the floor in front of me.

Suicide's demonic voice wrapped itself around me like a warm cloth on my icy forehead.

Call Him husband? Puleeze! You'll never have another man wanting you for a wife. You don't deserve that kind of happiness. And what's the point of going on if you have to go it alone? Because you do.

Have. To. Go. It. Alone.

And why not? Do. It. Who's gonna miss you? Even Sam will be better off with anyone but you for a mother. One little bullet. One little bullet standing between you and sweet relief. One little bullet to the head. Just think how warm the barrel will feel up against your temple. A quick squeeze of the finger, and it'll all be over.

I whispered a frantic prayer, "I need You, God. You've got to swoop down and clear my head of these lies. I need You to fortify my heart. Lead me through this moment into Your light. Forgive me for exercising my keen ability to pull things down into the mire in record time."

Another voice rang out, clear and strong: *Resist the devil, and he will flee.*

I chose resistance and kept up my desperate prayer. "Lord——I need You to get me through another day. Another hour. Another minute. Another investigation. There's too much riding on this for me to break down now."

I stood and moved to the windows, resting my forehead against the glass. Two young boys wearing bright blue and red windbreakers rode small would-be dirt bikes in tight figure-eights in the parking lot below. They'd pulled a wheel and a plank between two empty parking spots.

Blue Windbreaker Boy broke from the pattern and pedaled a large, fast circle around his cache. My heart beat faster as he stood up on the pedals, turned, and headed as fast as he could into the makeshift jump. The wobbling front tire gave him away—he wasn't going to make it. What he lacked in strength and speed, he made up for with his fierce battle cry. He was still yelling as he slammed into the board and hurtled head over heels across his handlebars.

I gasped, nearly turning away to run outside and help him, but his yowls turned into glee so fast it lifted my heart, and I started laughing too. His friend rushed over and fell on the ground beside him. He put his arm around him, and both sets of skinny shoulders shook with a kindred laughter. They pulled off their helmets and squealed even louder together.

I was smiling so hard my face hurt, and I turned around, refreshed.

My gun was on the floor where I'd left it. I snapped it back into the shoulder holster. All the power of heaven rejoiced when I bowed my head to thank the God who'd just answered a prayer I didn't know I needed: Insight into what needed to happen next to jumpstart this investigation flooded through me. I buttoned up my blazer, fluffed my hair with my fingers, and headed toward my waiting crew, humming.

Let's get this party started.

CHAPTER TWENTY-ONE

Friday, March 25

Heads swiveled and hushed tones filled the room before I started barking orders to the reluctant detectives. Garrett was the only one who met my gaze. For a third generation cop, he'd broken from family tradition and embraced both technology and the idea of female authority figures. Normally a friendly face in the crowd, his blue eyes held little warmth for me today. Friend or foe? Who knew? I turned my attention to him anyway.

"So give me the run down, Garrett. Top to bottom, and be quick about it." I nodded at him.

Seven detectives remained in the bullpen. Ralphie Contron and Dick Trent stood in the back, whispering. Where was Schlichting? The three stooges were insufferable, and inseparable. I would be grateful for the reprieve. And a tad suspicious of the timing of his absence. *He just happens to go missing the minute a DB shows up? And he has access to the station's photo paper, and he hates me. And he's one of just six who were at both crime scenes.* I tucked that thought away and focused on the now.

The remaining dynamic duo was annoying enough. They'd both been passed over for promotions three times. Bitterness hung in the air between them. Garrett cleared his throat and cast a nervous glance to the back of the room where they stood.

"We know Derrick Deter was a perp of the worst kind. Convicted sex offender for a veritable cornucopia of child offenses. Brought in for questioning for countless other cases but was never charged. He did time in four joints in three different states over a period of fifteen years. Got paroled early for good behavior each time. Picked up by the same woman at each release. Turned out to be his mother. Nobody's missing him—except her. Maybe." Garrett flipped on an LCD projector.

"So, how'd it happen? How'd he get popped and beaten to death in broad daylight and no one hears or sees a thing? This ain't exactly

Detroit." Impatience laced my voice. Not the first time. Probably not the last either. Garrett didn't seem to mind.

"We think he was stalking another group of kids. Following the same pattern. This equipment was found in his bag at the scene." Garrett clicked the remote through multiple images of high-end photography equipment. A New Orleans-style Mardi Gras mask lay on the table next to one of the cameras.

"Wait. Back up. What's the deal with the mask?" *It's probably nothing. But everything matters, right?*

"It was just there with his prints all over it, just like the rest of the stuff. And in case that's not enough for you, we've got this." He clicked again and scrolled through a dozen screens showing close up shots of a tow-headed boy with strong features and sparkling blue eyes. And they were still sparkling. Thank God.

"We think he'd zeroed in on his next victim." Garrett lowered his voice and paused for effect. "But did he know somebody had zeroed in on him?"

Contron spoke up from the back, his right knee cocked at an angle, leaning against the wall with folded arms. "That's the million-dollar question. Who would've known he was even in the area?"

"He was a known offender. Anyone with time and inclination can get online and look for updates to the registry in their neighborhood. That's not unusual." Garrett's tone was defensive. He glared at Contron.

"Time, inclination, and a nasty little sledgehammer thing, though? That's seems pretty exclusive. Should narrow your list down quite a bit. And, going after a perp like that … feels female, doesn't it? Doesn't this feel like another female killer to you?" Contron stared straight at me.

"Got any other feelings you'd like to discuss, detective? Maybe like a little resentment? Like maybe you refuse to believe your chief is innocent and back here leading your recalcitrant carcass? You got anything else you want to throw on the table?" I straightened up, staring right back at him as I spoke.

He stared daggers back at me but kept his peace. *Coward.*

"No? Good. Then how 'bout you set aside your dislike of me long enough to focus on the real killer here?" I raised my voice for emphasis, enjoying the red flush spreading across his forehead.

"And any of the rest of you wanting to take issue with my leadership are welcome to reread the report detailing my exact whereabouts during the past several days—and specifically during the double murder of my husband and his girlfriend." Heat vaulted up my spine. *Del, sticking it to me from the grave? Forcing me to give up the anonymity of my shelter women to remain free to catch his killer? Get with the program, Josie. Stay in the game.*

"For those of you who don't happen to watch TV, you should go online. Where you'd catch the fact that there are video tapes on file with the state's attorney, proving my exact whereabouts the entire time the murders were being committed. Any questions?"

Ralphie's eyes sprang open, and he stumbled off the wall and into Dick Trent. The clatter broke the tension in the room, and I smiled while my ironclad alibi rang loudly through the heads of every detective in the room. Their body language relaxed, and they looked up at me expectantly, almost in unison.

Finally. They wouldn't have fallen in line so fast had Schlichting been present. *Thank You, God, for small favors.*

"So, who else would've known about Deter?" The atmosphere had changed. Energy flowed throughout the room, and it was time to take full advantage of it.

"His victims. Any neighborhood watch types. Vigilantes. Disgruntled former co-workers and family members maybe. Creep like that mighta had enemies anywhere. Not to mention social and local services." Trent slinked to his desk in three strides and flipped open his laptop. I nodded my approval. He was following a good line of thinking.

"And if he had been hooked up to local services, that opens a whole new list of people who may have had access to his records, right?" Something was niggling at my subconscious.

"Right." Trent kept his eyes buried in the data before him. "Such as county health department and free clinic services. Think of the resources wasted on that guy while he was alive. Not to mention what we're still putting in with him six feet under. Now who's the crazy one?" He grunted and shook his head.

"Wait a minute. Crazy, huh?" *Crazy like a fox.* "Search under psych and social, and see who he might have been checking in with. Was he seeing anybody regularly? Maybe we can get a warrant to peek at some of his court-ordered mental health providers' notes?" A dim light turned on somewhere deep inside my mind.

"Whoa—that's weird." Trent looked up, wrinkling his nose.

"What? You dig up who he was seeing?" His drama was getting on my nerves.

"Yeah." His eyes met mine.

"And?"

"And I ... I don't know what to make of it."

"Maybe we can help." My eyes rolled before I could stop them. If he didn't start talking soon, I would reach out and slap him across the face to jumpstart his brain. "Maybe you could do us the supreme favor of using your words." I wasn't even trying to stem the tide of sarcasm flowing through each syllable.

"He *was* seeing someone regularly. Court assigned. Since his last incarceration ending in early release nineteen months ago." He was typing as he talked.

"Yeah, nothing unusual so far. Keep reading. And see who else might've been seeing the same shrink at or around his scheduled appointments. I know it's a long shot, but heck, you never know. We might get lucky. Stranger things have happened." I shoved a hand into my uniform pocket. Maybe the Fun Size candy bar I'd placed in it before taking it to the dry cleaner would still be there. Nope.

Trent had paled noticeably. He'd stopped typing and was focusing his attention on a printer sputtering to life along the back of the room. The rest of the guys had stopped talking and were looking our way.

"I take it you found something?"

He nodded, looking over at the row of printers in the back of the room and back to me before resting his eyes on the floor. I walked over to the printer and picked up the paper just before it fluttered to the ground.

The print was unnaturally small. It took me a moment to decipher the times, dates, numbers, and codes. When I did, I read it again. And again. The third time through, the growing chill in my gut froze to a glacier, and the soft spot under my chin ached like it always did just before I puked.

Derrick Deter had indeed received court-ordered treatment the last time he'd been through the system. Interestingly enough, his treatment came from the capable hands of Doctor Kira Stoklavich. Weekly. Just as you'd expect.

Exactly one hour and fifty minutes after my own weekly session.

The dim light in the far reaches of my mind snapped off.

CHAPTER TWENTY-TWO

Friday, March 25

"Ain't that an interesting little coinkydink?" Contron had slithered to the front of Garrett's computer and stood there, slouching like a seedy gangster. Trickles of defiance leaked from his dull eyes.

"What, you gonna offer us the butthead special again today, Contron?" Garrett leaping to my defense in front of the guys? Now that was an interesting turn of events.

"Boys, much as I enjoyed my junior high experiences, let's just leave them in the past for a moment, shall we? So Mitch, what might this mean? Put it together for me." My own brain had gone all fuzzy and soft after reading the print out. What did it mean? Whatever it was—and there *was* something—danced a toe's breadth beyond my reach. If anyone could put the pieces together, it was Mitch.

"Well, you'd busted him, what—four, five times?" She'd moved over to the no-longer-little group of us clustered around Garrett's computer.

"Less than that. Way less—more like two. I only *wished* it'd been four or five. Mostly, I wished I could've gotten him off the street for good. Before something bad happened." My voice trailed off.

"Something worse than this?" Contron's voice was menacing.

"Much worse than this—yes. He could've put the hurt on other kids. Peter—think of Peter. He's *safe*. You think that isn't worth Deter's death a hundred times over? Heck, I'd have killed him myself to keep him from hurting another kid." That should not have left my mouth. But I couldn't take the words back any more than I could've stopped them from falling off my tongue.

It was true: I hated Deter. He had scarred families and ruined lives without an ounce of remorse. He escalated as he got older. His death was the only real way to know he'd never harm another child. Fireworks erupted as I pictured the scales of justice, and smiled. Deter'd earned the right to die. And what about Richardson?

"Mitch, dig up everything you can on Corey Richardson. Is there any connection at all between Richardson and Deter? I want to know where he was at the time of each murder and what else is lurking in his background. Garret, head up the foot soldiers. Let's make sure we talk to every neighbor, delivery person, family members, the works."

Heads popped up, and a renewed energy sparked through the bullpen. *Good.* I nodded at Mitch, grateful to pass her the baton, and make my escape. Weariness fell over me like an electric blanket. I had to get some rest or I'd fall asleep and never wake up. I headed down the hallway, toward the parking lot.

The light pressed in, and I scrunched up my eyes. Starbursts lit up against a black backdrop as a wave of nausea floated through my gut. Great. In short order, I'd be visited by the mother of all migraines.

CHAPTER TWENTY-THREE

Saturday, March 26

The shrill sound of my home phone snapped me out of a deep sleep. "Chief Oliver here."

"Josie." Nick's smooth voice poured over me like gold silk. My pulse quickened, and warmth shot through me, head to toes. And slammed into an impenetrable wall of ice. *What about Nick?*

I pushed the foul thought aside.

"Nick?" Did my voice sound as breathy as it felt?

"There's been another one."

"Another murder?" I'd known him too long not to know his shorthand.

"Another murder." Slower, relaxing into whatever he wanted to tell me.

"And?"

"And it doesn't look good." His voice warmed, but he seemed more detached with each phrase.

Hot Italian super-agent or not, he needed to get to the point before he stepped on my last nerve. "Does murder ever look good?"

"This one doesn't look good—for you." Staccato words thrown out of his perfectly chiseled lips.

"Nick?" *What was he hiding?*

"It's Schlichting." The urgency in his voice must've been a kind of glee. Dirty cops were the worst kind of criminal in both of our books, and we'd been tracking this lout at the station for months. He'd been impossible to bust.

"*Schlichting?* Our Detective Glenn Schlichting is the killer?" I yelled into the phone, right leg bouncing. I loved a good hunt—especially when we caught our prey. *Way to go, Nick!*

"He's dead, Jo. It feels like our guy, but the MO's off a little. Made it look like he ate a bullet. Just over the line, south of Kenosha. Since this could be our guy, and he's crossed state lines, I'll be officially making this a federal case and taking over."

"What the …?" It was all coming at me too fast to process. It was all I could do to focus, to recall his words well enough to fashion them back into a sentence.

"Schlichting? Dead?" Well, not *much* of a sentence.

"In your wildest imagination, could you see him taking himself out?" Nick put his FBI secret agent voice back on.

"Not a chance." My words were icy and firm.

"Exactly. And it looks like he took himself out with a department-issued Glock."

"You already said that." I sat on the edge of my bed.

"Just like *your* department-issued Glock." His words grew narrow, distant.

"But mine's been in the department safe since I turned it over." I stood up, stars dancing before my eyes, stomach growing light and queasy.

"Exactly."

"What does this even *mean*?" A long sigh eased out as I sat back down.

"It means I have to see you. *Now*." His voice had taken on the *he-who-must-be obeyed* tone. My throat tightened.

"No, it may mean a lotta things, but it doesn't mean that. Not now, Nick. Not while I'm working." *And not until I know I can trust you.* "It's way too soon. I'm just getting back into the swing of things. The last thing I need is …" This was still my police department, wasn't it? Was his interest professional, or personal? It was getting hard to follow the fuzzy lines between us.

"… Is to try to figure it all out by yourself." He ratcheted up his insistent tone. But not enough to wash out hints of his extreme hotness.

Down girl. That wasn't real life, and any romance between us happened long ago, in the Land of Way Before. All but forgotten, and it needs to stay forgotten. Was Kira back in his life? The last thing I needed was the enormous distraction of Nick, up close and personal. Not a great idea. *Not now, not until I'm certain he's in the clear on this.* And certainly not when I was in certain, uh, moods. Let's leave it at vulnerable, not exactly immune to his charms. And judging from the thickness of my throat and the warmth spreading through my belly, I was not in a Nick-proof state of mind. Definitely not. Might as well leave me alone with an open box of dark chocolate truffles.

"Jo? Where'd you go? Please tell me you took me with you." His laughter was low and seductive.

Explains why he's the super-agent man. Still … reading my mind, even through a wireless phone? *Focus, girl!*

"Don't flatter yourself. I've got murder on my mind." I kept my tone crisp, businesslike. Maybe.

His laughter returned, spreading the deep, rising heat through me like a smooth mug of dark hot chocolate laced with peppermint. What's he doing calling me about this murder? Why not Mitch?

"Really? I've got something else entirely on mine." He chuckled, deep and rich.

He knew. He knew the power he wielded over me.

"Knock it off, knucklehead. If you want to play the Fed card and run this investigation, it's going to be on my terms, on my turf. You've got to show me some respect in front of my men, or this is never going to work. You think you can handle that? 'Cause I really don't want you around if you can't. I'm serious. I could use your help, but not the drama."

I wasn't being fair, nor was I in any position to be making demands, but heck, I was the Chief of Police, and this was my department. So a little poetic license wouldn't hurt anybody. Right?

Nick laughed a little louder in response. His breathing deepened.

"If that's how you want to play it, Chief. I'm all in. Where shall we meet? Your place or mine?" He was smiling through the phone.

I snorted.

"Meet me at the Grab N' Go just over the border." A favorite old rendezvous we'd both frequented for business with various colleagues—in my case—and operatives—in his—over the years. And it would give me the option of sorting out my thoughts away from him.

"I won't grab if you don't go." He laughed, hung up, and texted me.

Meet you in 30, beautiful.

I thought of Richardson. And his strong dislike of cops, and his philandering wife. Could she have also had an affair with Schlichting? I called Mitch to review my motive theory with her as I dressed. Five minutes later, I was heading back to the station, lights on, sirens off.

CHAPTER TWENTY-FOUR

Saturday, March 26

Mitch stood in my office doorway, smirking.

"Sit, Mitch. You're going to need to." My flat tone drilled the words down deep. I sighed, staring at the cell phone on my glossy mahogany desktop.

"Chief?"

"We got trouble." I continued my trance-like staring at the cell phone. What, did I expect it to jump up and start singing out the answer to this killer riddle?

"Yeah?"

"Yeah." Dark ideas tumbled over one another in the far reaches of my mind. Snatches of truth from the murder scene photos swirled around, with connections I couldn't yet see.

"What kind of trouble?"

"One more murder—or a death at the very least. And it all keeps circling back here. To us. To me. And possibly to Richardson." *And hopefully not Nick.*

"*What?*"

"Not what, *who*. Schlichting." I snatched up the cell phone and rose from my desk. At the mention of his name, her eyes darkened. "He's dead, Mitch. Nick just called to say that Detective Glenn Schlichting was found dead this morning. Evidence suggests the idiot took his own life." Saying it out loud did nothing to enhance my belief. There were seven kinds of wrong at play here.

"*What?*" Mitch's mouth hung open. Not a good look for the stunning red head.

"I know. That's where we're headed. North of the border. To the Grab N' Go to meet Nick. He'll catch us up with whatever else he knows, and we'll go to the crime scene from there."

I pulled out of the parking lot and headed to the highway.

"And neither one of you wants to go there alone?" Mitch pieced it together.

Nick hated Schlichting almost as much as I did and had found creative ways to express his feelings over the years. None of that would bode well in the face of a murder investigation. If this was a murder.

"And if it is murder, and not a suicide, you're going to want to have solid alibis on either side of you." She stared at me for several seconds. *Wrestling with her doubts again?*

"I guess you could say that. Safety in numbers and all." I kept my eyes on the road, voice texting Nick we'd be there in twenty as we turned north.

Mitch looked at me for several long, quiet seconds. When she spoke, it was more of a whisper. "And then there were five."

CHAPTER TWENTY-FIVE

Saturday, March 26

Mitch and I spied Nick's SUV at the Grab N' Go and drove toward it. Sunlight glimmered through the trees, showcasing multi-jurisdictional cops as they scuttled about, just beyond the low slung building. Dim objects took on a ghastly appearance at the edge of the black and yellow tape surrounding what looked like a solid acre around a gray clapboard shack standing a hundred yards behind the Grab N' Go building. A small cluster of cops encircled a large mass on the ground which featured the khaki sleeve of last year's department-issued shirt, torn and blood-splattered.

So, we weren't just meeting Nick here to convoy to the crime scene; this *was* the crime scene. A known meeting place for both myself and Nick. This had to put some doubt into the 'innocent' column for us.

I eased the car onto the shoulder of the road and turned it off. Then I pulled my sunglasses out of my purse and slid them on. I offered a silent prayer for Schlichting and his family. Heading into the horrors before us might be manageable with Nick and Mitch by my side. Just barely.

We lumbered out of the car and walked toward the tape separating us from the group of officers standing in a half circle. Nick was in the center. The scene's commanding officer identified himself as Mike Torrez. He was a big man, clad in tan chinos, a navy blazer, and field boots. The moment his last name hit the air, he stepped away from us, back to his peeps. He was also a man of few words.

Nick nodded to us and walked over to my side.

"Look like a Fed to anyone else?" I kept my voice low and my head up as we edged closer to the officers. I wanted to keep my musings between the three of us. For now.

"Yup." Mitch agreed, a step behind me on my left.

"An angry one who's about to get angrier working for me." Nick stepped within a few feet of the men, waving the big man away.

"Uh-oh. Another good lovin' gone wrong in the workplace, Vitarello?" Mitch jutted out one hip and opened her jacket, giving Torrez the evil eye, just in case there was any doubt whose side she was on.

Torrez walked toward us. The agent next to him said something that made him stop, look up at Nick, then nod and turn away with a shrug. And just like that, Nick took control of the crime scene.

Mitch ascended a small knoll, leading the way to the victim's body. "He sure does have a way about him." Her voice was thick with admiration.

"Must have something to do with his secret agent other-life," I jabbed, making my way over the uneven ground.

Nick smiled and strolled on in silence next to me, leaving unsaid the fact that something about Schlichting's death connected to my department. *The Glock.* What if Nick wasn't only here for me? If the powers that be deemed it necessary to unleash all that is Nick on this investigation, then something more than his abiding affection was up. Something horrible and crossing state lines. *Or, was Nick the horrible thing?*

"Whoa." Mitch was the first to reach the ring of cops. They moved aside to let her in and widened the circle further as Nick and I approached.

"Is that a—"

"Note?" Torrez interrupted from where he stood a few yards away.

"Smashed knee cap?" Mitch retorted.

"A *what*?" The Fed's surprised tone alerted the others to attention.

"Look at his knee, the way it's bent at a ninety-degree angle." There was no better bird dog than Mitch.

"So?" Torrez's patience appeared to be in thin supply. Feeling one-upped by a female cop?

"So you notice anything a little unusual about it?" The excitement in Mitch's voice leaped into my stomach. "Why isn't the knee cap prominent underneath the pant leg?"

Mitch was seeing something the rest of them may have missed. After only a few seconds on the scene. We were here to gather information on the death of one of our own.

My eyes traced the line of Schlichting's body, starting from the hip down. He lay on his back with his left leg straight, as if he were standing on it, a dent in the fabric where his left knee should have been. What were the possibilities here? I trailed over to his right leg, sharply bent, to the clear outline of his kneecap.

Mitch took it all in next to me. "This whole tableau's messed up."

"Ain't it, though?" I crossed my arms, concentrating on the scene. "There's no sign of blood on his pants from any sort of leg wound."

"But plenty of blood on the exit and entry wounds to the head." Mitch's tone was skeptical.

"Do they really expect us to believe he shot himself in the head and then just happened to drop into a Saturday morning yoga position?" I whispered to keep our puzzle close to the vest for now.

Mitch grunted and waved me on with a tilt of her upturned head. "Of course not. This is a set up."

I nodded my agreement. "There's a message here, but I can't quite read it."

I shook my head and shifted into silence.

Schlichting. He'd taken up way too much space in my head during the past few months. He'd been assigned to my department against my will. We had a complicated relationship, one I'd been talking through with Kira in the hopes of defusing some of the tension and powerlessness I felt in his presence. My heart was an empty bucket. Now I'd never get to make my peace with him.

Pig though he'd been in life, even Schlichting didn't deserve this.

"It's not like the world isn't better off without him, Jo." Nick appeared at my right, legs braced against the contours of the uneven ground.

I snorted.

"From what I heard, he did have it comin'. I'll never forgive him for putting the squeeze on you—not even once he's six feet under. Guy like that needs to be double-tapped to the head, just to keep him from coming back." Mitch was placating me. Afraid I'd drift off and leave her standing alone in a sea of crime scene cops?

Nick cleared his throat, then turned and started walking to the SUV. We followed. "You've never heard the story of how Jo and Schlichting met?"

CHAPTER TWENTY-SIX

Saturday, March 26

"I've heard bits and pieces of it, and I've had enough encounters of my own with the guy to know the world is better off without him." Mitch stumbled.

I sighed. Might as well tell the story myself. Maybe something would jar my memory that could help solve the murder.

"Okay. It's not my greatest moment. But it is the day I started really disliking Schlichting. This was back when he was on the beat in my town, my own neighborhood, months before he started working for us at Haversport." I took a deep breath. Maybe they would see past my shame in the telling.

"I was waiting outside in my green shorts, black canvas wedges, and black matching—"

"You remember what you were wearing?" Mitch interrupted.

I ignored her. "Tank top. And my light-weight, dove-gray hoodie. It was freezing outside when the squad car pulled into my driveway. I had my arms wrapped tight around my chest. It was impossible to tell who was driving, but force of habit made me walk up to the car as he parked. I waited for him to scramble out and to attention. It never occurred to me how I must look to him—I hadn't prepared for the complete and instant dislike in his creepy brown eyes."

We reached Nick's SUV and stopped.

"I remember how angry his eyes felt, staring at me, while he slid out of the car and rose to his feet. I could tell he wanted me to give way, but I held my ground. I stood right there and watched him watch me."

A chill shook down my arms. The rapt looks on my comrades' faces told me they were still with me.

"Even back then, you could tell by his buzz cut and the way he walked that he had, at best, an unforgiving nature. His uniform was too tight. His gun stuck halfway out of its holster, wear marks on the leather from a lifetime of bad habits. His hatred for all things female oozed out of every pore. He looked over every inch of my body—clearly enjoying himself—as I stood in front of him, flash-frozen by indignation in my own driveway. He managed to curb his disdain long enough to openly admire my legs. Sound effects and all."

I left out the part about him landing his crude gaze on my thighs. I rose up on my toes to stretch, sucking in air, taking a break before the hard part of the story. I leaned against the door of the car, my friends in a protective semi-circle around me.

"You can't imagine how hard I willed myself to move, how I was regretting every choice I'd made so far that morning—mostly the one where I'd called the police to report Del's abuse. I could see this would *not* end well. I was disgusted with myself, with my weakness.

"I remember trying to find my anger, hating that it had fled sometime in the first five seconds of Schlichting's ocular assault. I kept thinking that this cop was not going to help me—no one was ever going to help me. That I'd have to figure out my life and my marriage on my own. Kept thinking I never should've agreed to get the latest episode on the books like some average Jane Citizen. It was a mistake."

My voice trailed off. Did I have the courage to share the next part with them? Did I even want to? I rested for a moment on the gravel, leaning up against the SUV.

"It wasn't so much what he said, at first. It was the way he said it. He all but hissed at me. 'Mornin', *ma'am*.'

"'It's ...' I managed to get that one word out before my voice faltered. I'd lost my cool, and I couldn't get it back. Not with him staring at me like a piece of discount beef. I fell into blaming myself, wishing he would pull his eyes out of my crotch, get back in his squad car, and back out of my driveway. But I just stood there, powerlessness crashing over me.

"Then he yelled, '*It's what?*' He pulled out a pair of reflective sunglasses and edged them on.

"I could see my hoodie in the lenses. My tank top blazed back at me in the sunlight, and I realized the half-zipped jacket showed the latest collection of bruises circling my throat."

Mitch laced her arm through Nick's, her eyes glistening. A single tear tracked down Nick's cheek.

"I stared at Schlichting, starting to feel numb as his tone narrowed to a sharp, threatening point. He said, 'So, what's the problem, ma'am? Or should I be talking to the man of the house?' He must've mistaken my squad car in the driveway for Del's. Then he said, all menacing, 'Gotta be married to a cop. You seem the type.' He got up in my face, and the hair on the back of my neck stood up. He seethed at me then. 'So, are you? The type? You a badge bunny?'"

The nausea crept up my throat as it had on that day. I reached for the driver's door of the SUV, opened it, and put my foot on the running board. The pose gave me enough strength to look back on how I'd gotten my nerve back. How the weight of his words—*the insinuation*—had fallen all around me, and my anger had risen up.

Fury had coursed through me—at the thought of being pushed around by this angry cop as I stood in the middle of my driveway, wearing shorts and wedges, at nine o'clock in the morning on Memorial Day. I finally found my strength, my voice, my legs.

When I drifted through hallways of battered women's shelters … floating past a sea of anguished faces … I used to wonder when I'd look up to find my own frightened eyes looking back at me.

"Chief? You still with us?" Mitch put her arm on my shoulder.

"Sorry!" I shook off the chilling memory. "After he pushed me around, it took me a minute to collect myself. So I closed my eyes, feeling the warm sun on my skin, and I drew strength from who I am and the women and men who depended on me day in and day out. My power, my best self, the woman I always aspire to be—returned to me. And finally, listening to him disrespect me on my own property started to really tick me off."

I stepped off of the running board and closed the door. I didn't need the protective barrier. These were my friends. And this was the good part of the story. *At last.*

"My brain and my mouth started working again, and I looked right at him and told him to stop talking to me like that. Now. His head snapped up at the tone of my voice. I can still see him, glasses pushed up, sneering at me, looking right into my eyes, and trying to run that foul yap of his.

"I didn't let that happen. I told him to keep his mouth shut and open that pad of paper, pull out his pen, and take down my statement. I told him once he had it, he was going to get back in his squad car and get out of my driveway."

"I wish I could have been there for you. You shouldn't have had to go through that kind of humiliation." Nick had heard this story more than once over the years. Each time, his sorrow showed.

"No, but it had a happy ending. For me. The idiot swooped in toward me with his nasty breath hovering above my chest. But before he could touch me, I stepped back—enjoying it immensely when he lost his center of balance and stumbled forward. Then I pushed him with both palms in the center of his chest, hard."

"The dummy charged you?" Mitch's mouth hung open for a few seconds.

"Yeah. He spun around, furious, and came straight at me. But I didn't move a muscle."

"That's our girl." Nick had his arms folded across his chest. He seemed to be enjoying the retelling. This part, at least.

"And that's when we had a 'come to Jesus' meeting. I looked at him and said, 'Go ahead, you stone fool. Lay a hand on one of your own. Let's see how far your little manhood and your little badge'll get you then. Go ahead, 'cause I'm gonna enjoy every single second of this.'

"That's when the recognition crept across his broad face. The mix of hatred and raw lust in his eyes had finally been joined by real fear. And then I busted his chops, big time."

I sliced my hand through the air, leaning into them, egged on by the wide-eyed response of my friends. Were they proud of me?

"I said, 'What's the problem, officer? You've never seen an angry chief of police in denim shorts before?' I glanced at his badge and then back at his sweaty upper lip and said, 'Let me tell you a little secret, Schlichting. I know where you work. I'll know where you live before you make it all the way down my driveway, and I know your chief better than you know your wife. I could have your worthless head any day, any time. But, you know what? I could not be less interested in you or your badge. You just finish your report at the station. Get back in your teeny-weeny squad car, and get off my property. Then you go and spend some quality holiday time wondering what exactly I'll decide to do about our little encounter today.'

"Six months later, the guy had been transferred to my station, against my strong objections. Favors owed between two mayors." I shrugged.

"That's cold, Chief. Cool, but cold." Mitch's intensity burned in her eyes.

I held her gaze for a moment and then glanced up the hill toward Schlichting's body. "Well, it didn't turn out all that hot. For us *or* for him."

CHAPTER TWENTY-SEVEN

Saturday, March 25

We stood together in silence. Heat poured over my face and neck, but it was receding, bringing a welcome coolness in its wake.

Mitch unfolded her arms and placed her hands on her hips, calling out her inner cop. "Is it just me, or is someone going around eliminating some of our chief's worst enemies in a strikingly similar fashion?"

The words floated past me so I could examine them in fragments before letting them soak in too deeply. My pulse sped as the three murder scenes pieced themselves together. There had to be a sense of order. I had to create coherent thoughts and forge steel tracks to the next stop in this nightmare before another train wreck—before another murder.

"But that just can't be." So much for coherent thoughts. I shook my head, but nothing else came out.

"But it is, Jo. Look, I didn't buy the similarities theory before, but I do now. We'll have to wait 'til the crime scene boys do their thing, but we know what we're going to find. Don't we?" Mitch dug her feet into the soft earth, widening her cop stance.

"All three murder scenes do look to be connected." Nick's voice was softer than usual. It wasn't like him to use vague language.

"What do you mean, *look to be connected*? They didn't teach you better than that at Quantico? You don't *know* that they're connected, or are you just not saying what you know?" The chords in my neck strained under my skin, and my ears were heating up. *Where did Richardson fit in the midst of this theory?*

It seemed like we were at a funeral, my funeral, and everyone kept talking about how great the body looked. But hey, people, *I'm dead! How good could I really look? Dead don't look so good in my book!* I needed some quality time alone. I needed a safe place to sort this all out.

Nick stepped into my space, placing his finger under my chin before turning my face toward his.

"A word with you, Chief?" A wisp of heat flowed through me as I met his gaze. It melted away as splintered glass broke open in my stomach. Nick nodded his head toward his SUV, cocking an eyebrow at me.

Leave it to him to sense what I needed and to offer it—a little one-on-one with my favorite man-hunter. *Or was he turning his scope on me next?* I blinked and took a deep, settling breath.

"Looks like I'm riding shotgun with Nick on the way back, Mitch. Think you can manage the drive home without me?" I winked, tossed the keys toward her, and laughed as she snatched them out of the air.

"Whatever."

"Muttering does not become you." It felt good to get our banter back.

"Whatever." She turned and trudged to my car without looking back.

"Madame?" Nick held his arm out to me, and I took it. That familiar warmth oozed through me.

How could I even question my Nick? "What the heck? Do we believe in coincidences all of a sudden? Or am I in some kind of deep, deep trouble?"

Nick paused at the passenger door and opened it for me. Worry was etched across his face so deeply that chilling fingers tapped up and down mine. If I was hoping for reassurance, I was about to be disappointed. Badly.

He waited until I was seated and belted in before addressing my fears. "We're in it up to our eyeballs this time, Jo."

"Is it that bad?" He'd just spoken, but my thoughts trekked over muddy, sludge-filled rows of half-tilled soil.

His silence filled the front seat, accentuating the drumming in my head. I pressed my fingers to my temples in surrender to short blasts of pain sparking behind my eyes.

"I didn't sign up for this." I sighed and shook my head. Bad move. A subtle groan escaped my lips.

"Someone is and has been targeting you. You're being set up." His matter-of-fact tone forced its way around my heart and squeezed.

"Ya think?"

"Yes, I do. No one believes you killed Del and the woman." Nick's voice was all business. I loved him for that … and for not saying her name. "And the perv? The circumstantials put you two closer than six degrees of separation—but that's because you're you. And you made your views pretty clear." His driving was just like him—smooth and fast.

"And by *pretty clear,* you mean everybody and their brother could go on record to quote me saying how much I'd love to get my hands around his puny neck and choke the life out of him until he couldn't hurt kids ever again?" I turned my head toward Nick and slid down in the seat, stretching my legs.

"Yes. That was pretty clear. And pretty public." He glanced over at me, eyebrows raised. "And distressingly frequent."

"Yeah. Not arguing that point. But *everyone* wanted him dead. Any cop alive who had seen what he'd done to those boys would've wanted the same things, would've said the same things." I raised my hands, palms up, and stared at him.

"But you're the only chief of police on record as having said it. And not only to colleagues." He accelerated, moving left to pass a milk truck.

"Oh, yeah. That."

"Yes. That." He didn't need to fill in the blanks. There was TV footage of me saying the same thing into the camera, in the rain, at a crime scene. He swerved the car back to the right, blinker on and off.

"My judgment may not always be stellar."

"But you have a heart of solid gold. Unfortunately, it's not always visible."

"Hey now! I'm not that bad!" I sat up and gave him my full attention.

"Did you really tell Kira that you'd love to, and I quote, 'see that SOB rot in hell, the sooner the better' and that you'd 'like to be the one that puts him in the ground'?"

"Ah, well, it mighta come up. But those records are privileged. Just because she chose to share that with Mr. Handsome Secret Agent Man, doesn't mean anyone else will ever see them. That's a need-to-know kind of comment. And as far as I'm concerned, no one else needs to know."

"I didn't talk to Kira." He kept his eyes fixed on the road straight ahead.

"Then how?"

"Flick of the wrist. If I can gain access to your confidential records online with the help of one of the newbies in the Computer Crimes Commission as easily as I did, any prosecuting attorney worth their salt will find a way in too. And so could an average teenage hacker." His voice was steady, even. He kept his eyes trained on the road ahead.

"So, someone has targeted my known enemies and killed the four people I'd most love to see dead. And they've left breadcrumbs any toddler could follow to all three crime scenes."

"So far."

CHAPTER TWENTY-EIGHT

Saturday, March 25

Gray, hooded shapes wielding scythes and spiked clubs pulled victims through black, mist-shrouded trees in my hazy mind. Moss-covered stones lined my stomach. My head wobbled like a wrecking ball on a rusty chain.

A pasture full of newborn foals galloping by my passenger window snapped me out of my internal descent.

I swiveled my neck to give Nick my full attention as he drove.

"So, we've got some whack job on the loose, killing in my name. Only the real signature we've found so far happens to be the choice of the targets. Culling victims off an imaginary list similar to one only I would create. Talk about your invasion of privacy! And I thought spy drones were bad." My tone sounded forced, even to me.

How much more did Nick know? Were there new details that would strengthen the beliefs of the multitude of garden-variety cops hungrily clinging to the notion that I'd suddenly unhinged and gone on a killing spree? Did I even want to know?

"This is where you might want to speak up and share anything else you know. Preferably something that will point suspicions elsewhere. If you have anything. Anything at all." My hands emphasized what my mind couldn't quite verbalize, all but finger spelling to underscore my point. *Talk to me, Nick! Don't give up on me!*

"Desperation is not attractive—not even on you." Half his mouth smiled, giving him that Cary Grant appeal as he pulled into the parking lot of the Rocking Horse Lounge.

I turned to him, eyebrows arched.

"I thought you might like to talk it out." He put his hand out, waiting for mine.

The moment our hands met, he wrapped his fingers around mine. I closed my eyes, drinking in the warmth. *Safe.* I drew his hand up, pressed it against my cheek, and let it go.

Tension fell away from my temples, eased down my neck. I smiled. Mitch pulled in just as I was getting out of the SUV. And there, across the lot, sat Gino's gleaming Z28. We threw each other a nod and headed up the wooden steps.

Stale beer and cigar smoke greeted us as we pushed past a curtain of heavy beads on our way to the bar. Sawdust covered the floor. The red vinyl covers adorning the bar stools had seen better days. War-torn bistro tables with taller stools were scattered between the bar and the pool table. We claimed a four-top and ordered a pitcher of diet pop and a pot of coffee. Gino's booming voice heralded his arrival.

"M'hija, while this is a dark day for some, the light is about to dawn all around us. But first, we eat." He set down a tray loaded with breakfast plates, complete with napkin-wrapped utensils, and placed them around the table.

Gino set the tray on a tabletop behind ours and joined us. "Bon appetit, amigos. And for those of us who may have a bird-like appetite for food and a voracious appetite for information, perhaps you would like to feast your eyes on this." Gino pushed my untouched plate aside and replaced it with a large manila envelope. "You had another special delivery back at la hacienda. I managed to get a set of copies for us to review together. *Cuidate*, m'hija."

I gave him a puzzled look and opened the envelope.

I pulled out another envelope. This one was a quarter of the size of the other, compact, and white. "More photos?"

No one spoke. Nick frowned and handed me his butter knife. I pried the envelope open, pulled out four glossy, black and white photos, and placed them on the table. My nostrils flared, and I sucked in as much air as I could. White noise roared inside my head.

Pushing myself away from the table, I walked over to the wall and braced myself there for several seconds on shaky legs. I took a few deep breaths and stretched up straight, waiting until my heartbeat slowed to a fast trot before I pushed past the swinging doors to catch a breath of fresh air.

Five minutes later, I retook my seat at the table. All the dishes had been cleared. The photos lay out in order around the table. Everyone looked up at me. I gave a slow, small nod and sat down again, expelling a long, heavy breath.

"Now, just what on God's green Earth is this? And what are we going to do about it?" My words jarred my senses back to order.

Mitch's eyes were shiny with tears. She was like me—we both soldiered through horrific scenes in the moment. But our emotions always showed up later. Gino stood behind her, one protective hand resting on her shoulder. He put the other hand on my shoulder. Nick slid his stool over close enough so that our shoulders touched, like puppies crowding into one another for warmth and protection during a thunderstorm. *I can handle this. I've got my pack.*

Each photo depicted one of the three murder scenes, spotlighting the victims. Nick picked up the shot of Del and his girlfriend and studied it out of my field of vision. He placed it back on the table, face down, and picked up Derrick Deter's shot.

"Anybody else notice the two things that turned my blood to ice?" He pulled his gaze from the photo long enough to look each of us in the eye for a few seconds.

"*Sí, mi amigo*. Only, I think we have all noticed *three* things of great concern." Gino was holding the fourth picture. I couldn't piece together who was featured in that shot.

Nick looked up at Gino and frowned. Had he missed the third thing? "Each one of the victims of our three murder scenes is represented in the photos, and they're not tech shots. They had to have been taken by the killer." Nick spoke slower than usual, as if hoping one of us would finish his thought out loud. We didn't. "And all of the victims are still alive in the photos. Barely, but clearly still alive."

"Right. There's movement in these pictures. It's as if the killer said or did something to make them move right before taking the shot. Schlichting's hands seem caught in mid-air. It's like he was trying to sit up." I was focused now, buzzing with awareness.

"See that?" I pointed to an image in the dirty glass windowpanes on the shack behind Schlichting.

"What is that? Is that ..." Mitch's whisper set my teeth on edge.

"Yeah. A reflection. It looks like the killer isn't very big. And she's got a lot of hair."

"And a sledgehammer." Nick's voice was low, cold.

"Yeah. Looks like it." Mitch, leaned in, shaking her head.

"Either that, or she or he is wearing a wig. Let's not get tunnel vision and limit our options." We had to be missing a whole lot more.

The pictures were fresher than death—they caught the terror of the victims right before they died. Del and the other woman, bloodied, eyes dull and pleading. Del's mouth hung open in impotent debate. Derrick Deter, propped up against his van in the parking lot, two freshly smashed legs and one black eye, staring into the distance and not right at the camera. Schlichting's puzzled eyes looked straight into the killer's lens. But there was something different about the fourth photo.

Nick and Gino exchanged glances, and at Nick's nod, Gino placed the fourth photo, face up, a little further apart from the others. "And these are copies. The killer must've wanted you to see them. But who could know how soon you would see them? Unless this monster also has friends on the force?"

"Richardson's beginning to feel like a one off to me. A rogue cop maybe? Too soon to say. All we have for sure are three murder sites. Three sets of victims, each depicted in the perp's macabre photos." Nick had taken on the role of leader again, gesturing to the photos. "We know these four are dead, and we know how they died. But, what we don't know is anything at all about the woman in the fourth photo. Who, as far as we can tell, was very much alive when this picture was taken." Nick picked the shot up and held it out for all of us to see.

The last photo was hard to decipher. It was grainy, blurry, black and white. No time stamp, no date. It revealed a stern-looking woman seated in a straight-back chair in what looked like an office, but could have been a cubicle—too fuzzy to tell for sure. She had one hand on a phone at her ear, the other on the keyboard of a desktop in front of her.

"So who is she, and how much time does she have left?" I took the photo from Nick and held it in front of me. The woman's features were completely obscured. Why? Who was she? Why had she made the killer's list?

"What are we looking at, compadres?" Mitch would go all cop on us, helping us move from the soft side of our hearts to the stone-cold man-hunters we had to be. We needed her leading right now.

"These photos were delivered to you, m'hija, after you left last night. By courier, paid via a gift card bought with cash. Thus completely untraceable. The way the envelope was marked bothered the receptionist, and she called the commander on duty. He opened them, catalogued them, and they were entered into evidence last night." Gino was gathering the photos up and placing them back into the envelope.

"And our close personal friends in evidence sent a file to Nick, and he had you print them on the way to see us this morning, is that about the size of it?" Mitch's voice flowed with chastisement and admiration in equal parts.

"Something close to this, sí." Gino was not displeased with himself.

"So, safe to assume we're all thinking, we're all *fearing*, the same thing about the woman in the fourth photo?" I cut to the chase. I *had* to. The crêpey threads of my nerves started popping.

"She's everything different from the others." Nick nodded, tapping a finger on the Formica tabletop.

"She's alive, for starters." Mitch moved a hand to her hip and leaned forward. "Making this anything but a pre-murder shot."

"*Por cierto*. This is no death shot. This, this is surveillance." Gino crossed his arms in front of his chest and sat back, narrowing his eyes. "This is the strongest message we could receive from the killer."

My face scrunched up. A new set of worry lines started settling in. "Sure, right. I got it. I just don't know what that message is, G." I turned to Nick. "Do you?"

"Oh, yeah. And it's coming through loud and clear." He ran a hand through his silky curls.

"I get the loud part, but not the clear."

"'Come and get me. The race is on.'" Nick stood and stuck his phone in his pocket.

"And don't spare the horses." Mitch was up and on her way out the door.

A cold wave washed over me. I turned and followed them out of the dark bar and into the hunt.

CHAPTER TWENTY-NINE

Saturday, March 25

Nick reached the passenger door of his SUV and had it open by the time I caught up. Gino and Mitch were fanning out across the parking lot, heading for their cars.

"Guess I'm riding with him." I stabbed my head in Nick's direction and slid into the seat. My cell phone buzzed as Nick shut my door.

"Jo Oliver." My voice was heavy, unnatural.

Static jammed my ear, spiced with labored breathing. My shoulders quivered.

I drew the phone away from my ear to check the caller ID. *Mom.* I sighed. "Mom?"

Cement churned through my belly.

"I know you're there, and I want you to know I love you. Whatever you need, I'm on it, and I love you. Okay?" Tension edged down my shoulder into my bicep, begging my hand to loosen the death grip I had on the phone. I listened as she breathed into the receiver and waited for the words that would not come. She rarely spoke on the phone, but she'd called. Why? A single tear slid down my cheek.

"I love you, Mom. I'll take care of you. Just sit tight. It'll be okay." Stiffness rolled down my body from straining to catch any message she was willing me to hear. The call ended abruptly.

"How is she?" Nick stared at the road. We'd already crossed the line back into Illinois.

"Not so good." I drummed my fingers on my phone. "Hang on, gonna make a quick call." He took a sharp turn, and I had to hold on for dear life while punching in the numbers.

"Riverside. This is Cindy. How may I help you?"

"Cindy, hi. Jo Oliver here." I did my best to smile through the phone.

"Chief Oliver. You must be a mind-reader. I was just going to call you." Her business-like voice filled me with apprehension. She only snapped into professional mode when something wasn't quite right.

"What's up?" I tried to keep my voice pleasant. Or at least in the non-shouting range.

"Well, you might want to stop by sooner than later, if you can. Your mother's okay, but she's not as active as we'd like lately." She was choosing her words carefully. Too carefully.

"And?" *Get to the point!*

"And we think maybe you should consider having her reassessed. It might be time to talk about adding more memory care to her daily routines." She could have been reading from a script. An expensive script.

"I'm open to that. I'll call her doc and get the ball rolling. Get her on the books for another assessment." Which meant I'd have to take her to and from said assessment. When was I going to have time to do *that*?

"That would be great. I know you're busy, so I don't want to keep you. Let me know when you've got things set, and we'll do all we can to help make it happen." She was dripping in relief.

"Will do. And Cindy? Thanks for all you do for her."

"That's my job. And besides, we love your mom. She's a hoot."

I ended the call.

"What, pray tell, is a 'hoot'?" Nick turned toward me, a smile edging over the side of his face.

"I've got a better question. Where are we going?" Rows of cornfields streamed by on either side of the two-lane road we were on. Not a highway. Familiar territory, though.

"Just making a little stop on our way back to the station." He eased up to a stop sign, turning right toward the small town that had grown up on the banks of the Fox River decades before Riverside Senior Living Center existed.

"A little stop? Like a pit stop, maybe?" It was now obvious where he was headed ... and that we didn't have that kind of time.

"You could say that." He guided the car around a combine ambling down the road, nodding at the farmer as we passed. "More of a house call."

"You're a saint, but we gotta get back to work."

"Ever consider the possibility that we work as we go?" He pulled into the parking lot of a large yellow building. A small sign designated the spot we were in as reserved for the employee of the month. *Great.* They'd love that.

"Uh, not really." I stared at him, waiting for him to shut off the car. "Ever consider the possibility that we have no time left to figure out how to catch the killer before that poor woman moves from the 'pre' to the 'post' photo pile?"

"That's all I'm considering." He opened his door and slid to his feet.

"Huh? What, are you going to tell me you're about to do your best work while we visit my barely-there mother? You're making less sense than usual. What's going on in that mega-mind of yours?" We headed into the building. "What are we doing here?"

"Taking our best shot." He pulled the door open.

"Morning, beautiful." Nick bent down to kiss the cheek of a vibrant-spirited woman with sparkling baby blues that matched her cardigan. A crimson swath washed over her regal face. How long had she been sitting in her wheelchair facing the double doors today? Was someone coming to see her? I offered up a quick prayer for warm arms wrapped around her. Then I bent down and gave her a half-hug. She smiled at my touch, following Nick with her eyes as we passed.

"You should stop over here a few times a week and just do that." I linked my arm through his and led him down the hall.

"If it means I'd earn a little more time by your side, count me in."

Ceci, my mother's day nurse, stood at the nurses' station. In her dark blue scrubs, she stood out against the pink and white floral wallpaper. Beyond her stood a row of filing cabinets. A small, ornate wooden frame contained a matted display of elegant white script against a black background. Probably some perky dime-store saying. Were any of the residents able to read or remember it? Not my mother, that was for sure.

"Thanks for gettin' here so quick, Ms. Oliver. And for bringin' his hotness." She blushed and smiled at us like a high school dean might at a couple she caught necking under the bleachers. A smile I was very familiar with.

"How's she doing? Any more falls?" We didn't have much time. Something had to have happened for a staff member to say she was about to call me, and we needed to address it and get back on the road.

"Well, that's just it. We're not sure. None of us seen her fall, and she'd been a little more independent lately. She'd been walking up and down the halls and even going to meals on her own until this week." Ceci shifted her weight, jutting out one beefy hip. She looked down at the floor and back up at me. "There's been … looks like there mighta been some unexplained bruises in the past few days." Her gaze fell again as soon as she stopped talking.

"So, what's your gut telling you? More than a shower incident?" I kept my tone calm.

"She hasn't had another shower scheduled since you were here three days ago. And one of the bruises is, well, it's … it's just suspicious. I could get in trouble for telling you this, but you've been so good to my boys and my Billy, I just had to." She rushed this last bit out.

I put my hand on her arm and lowered my voice to a whisper. "What's going on, Ceci? What's so different about this one bruise?"

She still wouldn't make eye contact. A tear fell down her cheek. "I, um, I really need this job. But you need to watch after your mom."

Another tear escaped. And then another.

"What am I watching for? What did you see that's got you so afraid?"

"I didn't see any *one* thing, but I hear things. I hear a lotta things. And I do see some things … sometimes. And what I did maybe see, well, I can't be sure." She raised her head and set her moist gaze square on mine. "But that bruise? It looked an awful lot like a handprint. And I don't know no more trouble than that."

Convulsions rippled through my gut, and an iron vise wrapped itself around my head. We'd been investigating complaints of alleged rough treatment at the hands of Angela Murray, Riverside's director, but she'd come up clean. I hadn't seen anything suspicious, or I'd have cleared my mom out of there.

I'd had a hard time making the decision whether to pull her out of there or not, and I'd turned to Kira to help me think it through. It was one of the few sessions where I'd left with clarity around a decision I was grappling with. Mom stayed. No place was perfect and I loved the care overall. *Dear God, what have I missed?*

I dropped Ceci's arm and lurched down the hall to my mother's room, Nick by my side like a whisper. Two quick knuckle raps yielded no response. We pushed through the doorway together.

The hum and whoosh of the oxygen machine greeted me like an old friend. I followed the line into the bedroom and gazed down at my sleeping mother. One stick-thin arm lay out of the covers by her side. Papery skin clung to impossibly small bones. Age spots marked her hand, and a large bruise began above her wrist and spread all the way up to her elbow. Ugly, dark, tubular shapes marred her arm as if four large fingers had fanned out and savagely grabbed it. My eyes traveled up to her shoulder where the skin under her nightgown was discolored near her neck. *What the…?*

Nick laid a reassuring hand on my shoulder as I leaned forward to get a better look. Midnight-blue bruises rimmed the skin in front of her throat and on her right clavicle. I caressed her bony shoulder as tears filled my eyes.

Nick whispered, "I'll be right back. I've got a little something in my trunk that will give us another set of eyes when we most want it."

I nodded and squeezed his hand, sinking into the beauty of his presence in my life at just the right time. At all the right times. Sinking into the warmth of this incredible man who always had my back. How could I have doubted him? Why did I always have to mess things up between us? *Not this time. Not today.*

"Thank you." I held his hand against my cheek. "Just … thank you."

The oxygen machine shuddered. Something had changed in the pressure. Mom must be waking up.

CHAPTER THIRTY

Saturday, March 26

"Mom!" I knelt beside her. "How are you feeling? You remember Nick?" I turned to look over my shoulder, but he was already on his knee, one hand grasping my mother's hand. *What's not to love?*

"*Bellisima.* Run away with me." He leaned over and kissed her hand. "While I've loved your daughter since the day I met her, I've loved you just as much. How are you doing, and what's going on here?" Nick cooed at her, his olive skin shimmering in the dim light of the room.

My eyes moistened. "Mom, did someone grab you? Has anyone hurt you? Have they laid a hand on you?" There must be phrases she might respond to. I had to unlock a memory, an impression, anything.

Her rheumy blue eyes clouded further. Wispy brows furrowed while she worked her lips. A slow tear slipped down her cheek.

"Easy, bellisima. It's okay. We're here with you now, and we're not going to let anyone hurt you again." Nick lightly brushed greasy hair away from her eyes.

Was she being properly cared for? How much had I been missing while wrapped up in my job and the drama of my personal life? What else was going on here?

Her eyes closed, and she inched her hand over to rest on Nick's arm. I stood, watching the two of them, on the verge of tears. She opened her eyes, fixing them on me as she pointed a bony finger my way and fought to speak above the whir and hum of the oxygen machine. I nudged Nick over and bent closer.

"Catch her, Josie. You have to stop her." She rested from her work, letting her arm fall back by her side, eyes still trained on mine.

I cupped my hand around her face, whisking away a tear with my thumb. "Who, Mom? Who hurt you?"

"She did. The big one. The mean one." Her voice wisped through the air.

The big one. "The director, Mom? Angela Murry?"

"You know. You know her. You stop her." Her eyes closed before she finished sputtering.

I leaned down close. Kissed her cheek. "We'll catch her. Before she hurts anyone else." *But how many people are we hunting for?* A bead of sweat trickled between my shoulder blades, and my face flushed. Nick brushed past me, and I eased closer to her bed.

I squeezed my eyes shut and asked Jesus to call down angels of protection to set up camp all around her. I tugged open the drawer in the night stand next to the bed and found my mother's ancient Bible. I opened it up and peered down to read the first verse I found—from Isaiah.

> For I will contend with those who contend with you, and I will save your children ... Then all flesh shall know that I am the LORD your Savior, and your Redeemer, the Mighty One of Jacob.

Warm power flowed over me as I read the verses, first to myself and then out loud for my mom. The muscles in my arms and legs lengthened, relaxed. A lethal panther unfurled its graceful power within me. The power met my fury, sealing my resolve.

God, if the person hurting these defenseless seniors comes across my path, this monster is mine to capture and kill. I closed the Bible and replaced it in the nightstand. Nick appeared. We stepped away from the bed, and I took his hand in mine, turning toward the door. He stopped me, pointing to a spot above the door and then to the mirror facing her bed. Cameras. Good boy. That was fast. I grinned, nodding my head as we hit the hallway, our steps in perfect synch.

"Let's do this, Nick."

Faint odors of recent baths and "accidents" woven in with ammonia assailed us. Was this normal?

I looked at Nick and grimaced.

"Smells like compassion to me." He shrugged.

Three staff members clustered around the desk. *Shouldn't they be out checking on the residents? Is this normal?*

"Good morning, ladies. Anything new going on with my mother?" I couldn't stop myself from using my police chief voice. *Let's hope it gets us somewhere. I'm a step away from using a whole lot more.*

They paused a beat too long and looked at each other. The tattooed blonde answered first. "Uh, not that we know of. Like what?"

I leaned over the counter and touched her wrist. "Like anything you know of that might cause the severe bruising around my mom's neck?" My tone had gone from cop to lawyer.

Tiny beads of sweat broke out on the blonde's forehead. She looked at her comrades before responding. "Uh … well … you know how it is, ma'am …"

She wasn't new, but I couldn't remember her name. I made a show of looking at her plastic tag. "No, I don't. Why don't you tell me, *Pam*."

A loud beep erupted from the monitor behind her. A red light flashed, and a room number came up. *1214*. The women exchanged worried glances. At Pam's nod, two of them hurried down the hall. "*This* is how it is. We serve over seventy seniors here with varying levels of care needs. Some days are smoother than others. Everybody here loves your mom, and nobody'd want to hurt her. This is the first I've heard of bruising of any kind on anyone here, and I promise you I'll look into it. Would you like me to call you after I've spoken to everyone on shift in the last few days?" Her eyes hardened.

"Yeah, I would. I'd like that a lot. You know what I'd like even better? Chatting with Ms. Angela Murray. You've got all my numbers, right?" I leaned an elbow on the desk.

"Yes. And once Director Murray gets in, I'm sure you'll hear from her." The beeping erupted again. "Excuse me. I'm needed." She hurried down the hall.

Nick and I followed her on our way out of the facility. Room 1214 was the last door on the right. Muffled sounds were coming from the open door. As we got closer, a low moan wafted out. We both looked into the room.

Arnie, a large, wheel-chair-bound man, was lying on the floor. The three women were working him back into his chair. He turned his grizzled head in our direction. Recognition flashed in his cloudy eyes. We gazed at each other for several seconds. The women tugged at him in unison until they got him upright in his chair and began to buckle him in. A slow tear built in his one good eye and slipped over the lid. I nodded at him and turned away with stinging eyes.

What was really going on when no one else was here?

CHAPTER THIRTY-ONE

Saturday, March 26

We walked through the glass doors separating the assisted living area from the rest of the facility, pausing to look at each other when we reached the entrance leading to the parking lot. I checked my phone for updates; there were no new messages. *Good.*

Nick popped an eyebrow up. "What do you think? Go for it?"

"Oh yeah." I turned my head toward the main hallway that would take us to the front desk. "Might as well deal with it while we're here and hopping mad."

Nick adjusted his stride to match mine. "And while *I'm* here to keep you from killing the good Director Murray."

"I prefer to think of it as knocking some sense into her." I stuck my head into the café area flanking the hallway. Brightly colored streamers hung from the light fixtures. Plastic rabbits were stuck to the wall next to a painting of violets. Green, pink, and blue grass lined the tables, and the residents' name cards bore festive little carrots and eggs in the corners. A six-foot rabbit-man in a dark brown tux, with his paws out as if waiting for a tray, had been stuck in the corner. Easter on steroids.

"I prefer to think of it as a friendly drop-in visit, giving us a chance to share some information and gather a little intel." Nick hooked his arm through mine and guided me around the corner to the reception desk. It was abandoned.

"Must be on break." He stretched his long body over the desk, turned the appointment book upside down, and read it. "Training slash rep luncheon at Hermann's."

"Of course they're out to lunch. How convenient." I rolled my eyes.

"For us. Practically neighborly." Nick stepped back and looked at me. "So, beautiful, you thinking what I'm thinking?"

"Lead the way, and we'll find out." I looked around the room and stepped into the hallway we'd just exited. The place was empty. "Let's do it."

It took me several long strides to catch up to Nick. He was standing at the end of the narrow corridor behind the reception area. Two doors stood on either side of the hallway leading to the only door with a nameplate on it—*Angela Murray, Director*.

Nick tried the doorknob. Locked. He pulled a set of picks out of his wallet and had the door open in less than ten seconds.

"Smooth." I wasn't an amateur when it came to picking a lock, but I'd never make it to his status. Lucky for me, I had other assets.

"After you." Nick gestured me into the office and handed me a pair of blue gloves that looked suspiciously like the ones in a carton on the supply cart in the hall. I slipped the gloves on, and flipped up the light switch by the door.

We stood side by side, drinking in the details of the room before us.

"Stark." I stuck close to Nick.

"That's one word you could use." He turned to the left, closing the door behind us.

The director's L-shaped desk and executive leather chair took up most of the room. Two plastic-seated chairs that matched the ones in the café had been placed in front of the desk. A vintage gray metal filing cabinet stood to the left of it. "Utilitarian."

"That's a more interesting word." Nick moved toward a closet door. He stood there, not moving for over a minute—clearly having some sort of moment.

"This is unexpected." A plastic framed version of one of my favorite sayings hung on the wall behind Murray's desk for every visitor to see. It was a quote by Andrew Jackson, written in big black script. I read it out loud for Nick. "I was born for a storm, and a calm does not suit me."

"Where have I seen that before?" His voice sounded thoughtful, sincere.

"You're joking, right?" I turned around.

"No. There's something about it. Like I'm having a déjà vu moment. Something about the way the frame contrasts with the too-white wall behind it. The lettering in the last line. I've seen it before." He stood with one arm bracing the other, chin resting between his thumb and forefinger.

"Of course you've seen it before. It's on one of my favorite coffee mugs. There's your déjà vu."

"No. There's something else. Something more. It'll come to me."

"Well, while you're waiting for it, I'm going to take a little walk through this filing cabinet." It wasn't locked. My eyebrows flew upward. I pulled it open and started sifting through the files. "Here's Mom's file. One of them anyway. Looks pretty routine."

"Keep looking, beautiful." He was rummaging through the closet behind me.

"Not much here. Bills. Activities. Construction information for the expansion project. Nothing lively."

"There's something here. I can *feel* it."

Whoa. The 'following your gut' stuff wasn't like Nick at all.

I closed the last file drawer and straightened up. "What's going on?"

"Something. I just don't know what yet. There's something off about this room. It feels staged."

"*Staged?*" It was bland, I'd give him that. Spartan even. But staged? "So, what would that mean?"

"Who stages rooms?" He'd gone back into his thoughtful stance in the middle of the office.

"People trying to sell something. Like a house." I put the desk chair back the way I'd found it. Replaced my mother's file. Closed all the cabinet drawers.

"Right. Who else?" He turned around and closed the closet door.

"People trying to hide something."

"My point exactly."

CHAPTER THIRTY-TWO

Saturday, March 26

We maintained a shared meditative silence as Nick drove through familiar territory on our way back home. When we hit the city limits, he turned right on 120 instead of left.

"What's up? I thought we were going back to the station. Bit of a circuitous route, but still." I frowned.

"*We* aren't. *I* am." He kept his eyes on the road.

"Want to explain first or start the argument now? Good to go either way here." I loved Nick, but he was going a little overboard on the protective pseudo-boyfriend stuff.

"I'm taking you home. It's been a heckuva day for all of us, but the personal connection makes it ten times worse for you. You need a break." He still refused to look at me.

Uber controlling or a symptom of love? Hard to tell. Either way, time to nip it in the bud. *And what if it was something else entirely? Something much more sinister?* I gripped the door rest and turned to face him, seatbelt tightening against my chest.

"I appreciate the big brother stuff. I do. But I can't have you keeping me from living, breathing, and being who I am. Period. No excuses, no censures, no gate keeping, no judgment."

"Leave this case to us—sit this one out. For me. Please." He clenched his teeth hard enough for me to hear the tick of his jaw.

"I'm a cop, Nick. First and foremost when on a case—with you or without you. And I'm on the case of my life right now. So turn this boat around before I abandon ship. Your choice. Either way, I'm not bailing on this case." I shoved my hands into my jacket pockets. "Look, I appreciate your wanting to protect me. You're the best friend I've ever had."

Wrong word choice.

His face turned dark red, and the tick of his jaw resumed. "And you're so much more to me than you'll ever know." His soft tone carried sadness.

We drove through back roads toward Haversport in silence, reaching the city limits in under ten minutes. His Federal version of municipal plates working in our favor once again. He extended the silence as he pulled the car into the station's parking lot.

"Thank you." I reached over and squeezed his hand in an effort to repair the damage done by freshly slung arrows.

He did *not* squeeze my hand back.

"Back at the ranch. See you in a few hours maybe? I'm gonna go gas up. And I strongly suggest you take a nap on your office sofa. OK with you if we let Gino and Mitch give the team a few hours off, and then start the briefing at two?" He pulled the car up to the steps.

"Whoa, lovin' the convenience factor. Go for it." Was this an I'm-still-on-your-side kind of gesture? Or a distancing move? Either way, I was glad he wasn't trying to talk me into going home.

"Thanks, partner." I patted his hand before opening the door and heading into the station. I trudged down the empty hallways, picturing the creamy white sheets on the sleeper sofa in my office.

He'd done all he could to support me. He only wanted what was best for me, for us. Why did I feel like I was walking through a minefield at gunpoint?

Mitch and Gino were in the middle of the briefing when I walked into the bullpen, none the worse for wear after a quick shower and change in the locker room downstairs. Mitch had insisted on hiring Gino as a consultant on the case. His background in surveillance and criminal apprehension would come in handy.

They both looked up and paused. Detectives sat alongside at least half a dozen Feds, all gathered in a loose circle around the room. The room quieted as I leaned against the back wall.

Whatever. I nodded at Gino and Mitch. "Carry on."

"Thanks, Chief. As I was saying, Schlichting makes the fourth vic that we know of. But there could be others." Mitch glanced at Gino, cuing him.

"Statistically probable. Likely well before this current spate of murders." Gino was playing big shot consultant today. No pronounced Cuban accent.

"What's the difference between a nexus and a trail?" Contron snarled from the middle of the seated pack.

"Excuse me?" Mitch was on it, one eyebrow cocked, lips pressed together in a vise grip.

"When do we stop ignoring the obvious and start vetting our free range suspects a little more?" Contron didn't turn around and look at me. He didn't have to. Schlichting's death hadn't improved his overall disposition.

I pushed off the wall and sauntered over to him, waiting for him to close his mouth. I put both hands on the metal back of his chair. He stiffened but wouldn't face me. I stood there for a moment, as blotchy crimson marched across his beefy neck.

"Do you really want to dance with me again, Ralphie? 'Cause I got a little question of my own for you. What's the difference between intellectual curiosity and insubordination?"

"About two weeks, unpaid." Commander Mike McCaskey piped in from the front of the group, breaking the tension.

I grinned and sent him a grateful look. He was old enough to be my father. It had taken me a while to prove myself to him. I still wasn't quite sure what I'd done that had finally won him over, but I'd been the grateful recipient of his respect ever since.

I breathed deeply as I made my way to the whiteboards. Mitch turned her attention back to the screen. The third of the four photographs we'd reviewed over breakfast hours ago appeared before us. Schlichting's brutalized body glared off the white background. A wave of dizziness lapped at the shores of my mind. Mitch flipped over to an empty screen. She hit a button, and the number '1' appeared before us. Followed by the name of a drug I'd never heard of until it had shown up in the tox reports for both Del and his girlfriend.

"What kind of mind are we dealing with here? What's the link between the victims? There are three distinct signatures that we know of so far that have been present at every scene. And according to my search engine, 'Scopolamine is a little-known drug used for motion sickness and vomiting, but it can also render the user open to suggestion and/or commands.'" Mitch put her phone down and paused, looking at the intense faces of the men and women in front of her.

"This some new designer drug? Or am I just getting too old to keep up with the jonesing ..." McCaskey's play on words evoked real laughter and a few eye rolls. This man had a fine mind disguised behind his Columbo demeanor.

Mitch looked him in the eye. "It's not new, it's just rare around here. Rare enough for us to send it out to university hospitals for ID'ing. But it's apparently used often enough in Venezuela and Thailand."

McCaskey leaned forward in his chair. "Okay, so we got an unusual drug. Maybe our killer knows her way around a hospital. Or spent a little time in med school. Or traveled out of the country recently. What else you got?"

Her way around the crime scene. Garrett had kept him up to date. They'd been partners for the past three years. Their solve rate was among the best in the state.

Mitch hit the button, and a photograph of a sledgehammer with dark red stains appeared. Looked like the one previously lodged in my fireplace. *Thank God for solid alibis.*

"A sledgehammer. It seems that our killer prefers to drug her victims. But in the first murder, she shot them in the knees. Why? Couldn't get physically close enough to drug them? Or had it been planned that way? Is this just standard evolution of an MO? How would the killer know there would be very few people around the day of the lake house killings? And even more troubling, how would she be able to get close enough to plant evidence in the chief's home?"

That was my husband she was talking about, reduced to a party in "the lake house killings." What would I do with the lake house now? *Focus, girl. Focus.*

"Maybe she knew them. Maybe it was a neighbor. Maybe she got lucky. Maybe. The only thing we know for sure is that our killer used a sledgehammer in every single murder. We ran a check on the make and model of the ones we've recovered and learned nothing more than that each one was a different brand. Probably purchased off the internet instead of locally."

"And then she planted the dang thing in the chief's fireplace? That ain't even smart, and it's gettin' a little ridiculous on top of it. How many more sledgehammers is this chick gonna go through? And where the heck else they gonna show up?" McCaskey spoke the words that everyone in the room had to have been wondering. "That poor louse

Richardson, even with his hospital tech background, he doesn't sing to me for any of this."

"And that leads us to the third signature element—ties to the chief." Mitch had one hand on her chin, lending her a professorial air.

McCaskey nodded. "Which Richardson does not have for anyone beyond the lake house killings."

Mitch cleared her throat. "Back to the ties. The first goes without saying. The second, Derrick Deter, is a man she's tracked and thrown behind bars on two separate occasions. And the third, Schlichting ..." Mitch's voice trailed off.

"Was dirty, and we all knew it. The chief was the only one with the guts to confront him. And she did. A lot. And suddenly he turns up as victim number three? Now ain't that convenient."

"And then there's the masks. Death masks maybe. I'm not sure. But, the first scene, with the fishing line mask. And Deter, an actual mask was left at the scene."

McCaskey leveled his eyes at me. "What are we missing with Schlichting?"

His broken body, the raised leg. "The pose. It *was* a yoga pose. But how is a pose a mask?"

"Too soon to say, but for sure we know he was posed. That in and of itself could serve as a mask. Masking the effects of the murder." His hands moved as he spoke.

I nodded my head. "It's possible. Puzzling, but possible."

Mitch coughed, and then resumed her presentation. "And here's the last piece to the puzzle for now. It's pretty gruesome. The three pictures you've seen on this PowerPoint came from photos that were couriered over to the station last night." Mitch paled a little as the room erupted into surprised shouts. "There was no note. But the message here is loud and clear." Mitch hit the button, and the fourth photo filled the screen.

"I ain't seein' it, commander." McCaskey squinted at the screen.

"Yes, you are. Assuming we're right, and the woman in that shot was still alive when it was taken, it follows that woman's shot was taken recently. She's very much alive, and the killer sent us a photo of her along with the four victims."

"Lord, help us all." McCaskey said. "It's like she's sayin' 'try and stop me.'"

"Yes. It is." Mitch clicked her mouse a few times, and the screen went black.

Wait. What was that? There was something familiar about that last photograph. Before I could get the words out, Nick's confident voice floated up to the front. "Put that last shot back up. Would you please, commander? I think I've seen that office. In fact, I'm pretty sure I was in it a couple of hours ago. With the chief."

CHAPTER THIRTY-THREE

Saturday, March 26

Scenes of Angela Murray's office. Her chair pressing against a barren wall. *I was born for a storm, and the calm does not suit me.* All cylinders clicked at once. "The Jackson quote! That picture on the wall—it's the same one that's shown on the top of picture number four!"

Nick approached from the back, nodding his head.

"We were just there. Riverside. My mother's a resident in the Alzheimer's wing. There's uh … there's been some trouble there this week."

"Evidently." McCaskey was at it again. "Check this out." He held up his cell phone, reading a report. "Riverside's second-in-command just called dispatch. Apparently, Ms. Murray didn't show up for work. It took them a while to notice her absence, because her car was in her usual parking spot, and her calendar was filled with meetings. She's not responding to any of her phones and it's not like her."

I looked down at my phone, read the same message, and moaned. "Oh, no. Besides this woman maybe being taken, there've been indications of abuse. I have concerns about my own mother. Maybe our killer does, too. It looks like the killer's taken the Riverside director."

"I agree. But where? How long ago? How much time does she have left?" Nick pushed the podium to the side and stood in front of the whiteboard. He drew a rough outline of Paradise County and put four X's in different locations, one just outside the northern border. One of the X's was much bigger than the others. "Four bodies in three different locations. And Riverside is right in the middle of the kill zone. What's the killer trying to tell us?"

"And what's with the creepy photos?" McCaskey was on his feet, arms crossed. "Why start toying with us now? Why not start with the taunts earlier? What have we missed along the way?" He scratched his chin with a thick knuckle. "I mean, sledgehammer littering ain't exactly subtle."

"Right. But it *is* an unusually creative way to terrorize the chief. Think about it—framing her for her husband's murder, right off the bat." Mitch remained silent on the girlfriend part.

"And the sonuva—" I was just getting warmed up when Nick cut me off. *In front of the guys. Talk about your disrespect.*

"Each of the victims shares an intimate connection with the chief." Nick still held the red dry erase marker.

Intimate connection? What was he thinking? I waited for snickers to roll around the room. There were none. Maybe it wasn't noticeable. To a room full of detectives. *Yeah, right.* Another reason to think about making a different choice with Nick. *One of these days.*

Time to tune in. Nick was still droning on, with the occasional chirp from McCaskey. The rest of the staff in the room seemed fidgety, ready to hit the streets.

"You got any more enemies left, chief?" McCaskey looked at me.

Nick picked up the thread without missing a beat. "Let's put it another way, detective. Chief, if you were going to make a list of the people who might have the biggest ax to grind with you, who might that include? Think about it. Anyone out there you've arrested and thrown away that might still be harboring a grudge. Someone who could hate you enough to frame you for these murders? I was going to suggest the Mentor Sister Serial Killer, since he had accomplices. But he doesn't fit. Who knows you well enough to be able to create a kill list that looks like it came right out of your darkest fantasies?"

My head swirled, and I waivered on my feet.

Besides Nick? Gino? Donna? Mitch? Who indeed?

CHAPTER THIRTY-FOUR

Saturday, March 26

Tension pinged off the walls. Most of the detectives broke into motion, some jumping to their feet, some throwing hands through their hair, others pulling out cell phones, notebooks, pens. The blood was in the water, and we were on the move. McCaskey lost no time reading between the lines. "Isn't elder abuse one of the top ten issues for lawmakers on both sides of the aisle in DC and Springfield?"

Nick looked at me, ignoring McCaskey, and softening his tone. "And your mother's gonna be fine, what with you visiting her as much as you do. Right down the hall from a decorated vet we all know and love who experienced a strange episode while we were talking to the head nurse not quite three hours ago. There was a look of …"

Nick paused.

I didn't appreciate him answering for me. Between his open expression of our inner relationship, and his take-charge attitude, was this is the kind of man I wanted to let any closer to my heart? Was this sentiment an expression of my nerves? Or inner alert system kicking in? Why was I spending so much energy looking under non-existent rocks? Why couldn't I relax into the idea of having this great guy in my life? *Three hours ago, I was ready to walk down the aisle with Nick, and now just being in the same room with him gives me the heebie-jeebies. What's going on with me?*

"'Tragedy' is the word you're looking for." I'd never forget the look in Nick's eyes. Time to take back control of this investigation. Again. And let the love thing sort itself out later.

"Yes, tragedy on his face. Even without this new twist, I'd want to go back and see what's really going on. Something just isn't right about that place. Elder abuse isn't the only thing wrong down there." He failed to mention the surveillance cameras he'd already installed that would let us do exactly that, remotely.

"What are you waiting for? Saddle up and ride out there." God bless McCaskey for ignoring Nick and directing all attention to me again. Could I get him to join me for any future near-dates with Nick? To make sure I behaved myself.

"Alright, Nick, Gino and I are heading back to Riverside." A game plan formed.

Mitch stepped in before I could send out my teams. "I know you want to go back and check on your mom, and nobody's going to bring the passion to the table in tracking this director better than you right now. So go check on your mom while you interview folks out there. Two birds, one stone. You've given these muscle heads enough to do."

"Thanks." I nodded to Nick and Gino, and the three of us turned and headed out of the bullpen toward the parking lot exit. "Let's hit it, gentlemen."

Nick wedged himself in between Gino and me and slid his arm around my waist. I shrugged it off. "Gino and I are going to ride back to Riverside. I need you to follow up with your hotsy-totsy bad boy predictor program and add this new vic ID." It wouldn't change anything, but it sounded good. *Didn't it?* If nothing else, it was a face-saving way for Nick to hit the road and give me some breathing room.

He got the hint. He stared at me coolly for several seconds and then turned on his heel and headed toward his car, waving goodbye as he walked away in silence.

This would give me a good reason to dump all my irrational fears of commitment out on the dashboard for Gino to dissect and reassemble on our way.

He cocked an eyebrow at me. "*Es cierto* that we have much to discuss."

I managed a snort and a nod. "Let's just put it this way, my friend—I wouldn't mind a little friendly advice on the Nick front."

Gino was a master at figuring stuff out, especially with matters of the heart. But back to the case, I was interested in anything that could get us any closer to saving someone's life—even if, in my own personal economy, I didn't think they deserved saving. "Plus, I'm looking forward to hearing more about your new geo-locator toy."

"If only you were half as eager to spend time on spiritual matters." Gino grinned at me.

"Well, let's hope I'm in the mood for that, too." I'd been struggling with the concept of God being present in my life when it just kept going straight down the toilet. I knew God loved me and had a plan for my life, but I just wasn't seeing how His goodness was reflected in the crap conditions I'd been served up ever since He came into my life. Gino had been trying to talk to me about trusting God in the midst of my circumstances, but I'd been avoiding the subject. It'd be more refreshing to talk about another business success in the colorful life of one of my dearest friends.

Gino must've been making some serious bank on this one. You'd never know it by looking at him, though. He kept most everything he did on the down-low. Except for his faith, and his choice of hot little sports cars, of course. And then there were his stories of a host of orphanages, schools, and church plants all over the world he seemed to bankroll single-handedly. Would it kill a guy to talk a little more about killer-hunting technology and a little less about suffering for Jesus?

Much as I respected him for his habitual self-sacrifice on behalf of others, I was dying of curiosity about his professional world. But Gino had his own timetable. His stories included what he thought I needed most, when he thought I was most open to hearing it. More often than not, his twenty-first century espionage skills took a back seat to the gospel. *Fair enough. First things first.*

CHAPTER THIRTY-FIVE

Saturday, March 26

Gino led the way to his black SUV. He'd had it tricked out with lots of security features, most of which were borderline legal in this or any other country. When would I have time to have him walk me through the special upgrades?

He held the passenger door open for me. "Señora?"

I air-kissed his cheeks and got in, smiling. He headed us back down Highway 120, well-acquainted with the route. Gino was my mother's most gracious and patient visitor. It must've irked him to think there had been something going on under our noses for quite some time. It sure bugged the heck out of me.

"You must tell me all that is going on between you and your good saint Nicolas. He remains as handsome as ever, and yet you seem to have grown a little cold. Why is this so?" Gino doubled down on his accent.

Must've been gearing up for a real good lecture. One I'd just as soon miss. *Fat chance.* "I can't have him coddling me in front of the guys, for one. Heck, I can't have him coddling me period. I mean, I get it. I do. There's a lot of crap going down in all directions, but I like to think I handled it all alright before he came along, and that I'll handle it all just fine the day he drifts off in the middle of the night."

"Ah. That is the whole enchilada, m'hija. *Tienes miedo.*"

"No, I'm not! I'm not afraid. I'd call it more a low-grade, ever-present annoyance. But if I was, what would I be afraid of?"

"Death. Death by falling in love, having to trust a man again, of having to dive in and see whether or not his arms are strong enough to support you both." Gino slipped on a pair of mirrored sunglasses.

"But what if what I need right now is a little time alone? Fewer arms, more solitude? I don't know if I want to jump into a relationship with Nick right now, G—it's too soon. I don't even know who I am anymore. With Nick or without him. With Del or without him. I just don't know."

"That is why you must seek the Lord in prayer. He will lead you, but you must go to Him first. He wants nothing more than for you to delight yourself in Him." Gino was on a roll.

"But if I can't trust a man, how can I possibly trust God?" *There it is.*

"M'hija. God loves you. And He is not a man. He will never break His promises. He is the same today, yesterday and tomorrow. And I believe His plan for you will include the perfect man for you. Maybe even an Italian." He winked.

"So, that's what? A push in the Nick direction? Again, not so fast, not so sure. And please don't get me started on the will of God. I've been praying and asking Him for guidance. I swear I have. So far, I got nothin'. All I know is, I'm on edge. Seems like it's time for me to make a decision. And I'm leaning toward taking a break from Nick." The last row of cornfields flew past us. We'd be at my mom's very soon.

A slight smile crept across Gino's face. His profile was regal and uncompromising, like my father. When was the last time my father had even called my mother? He knew she was here.

My father was a multi-decorated vet and something of a rogue himself. He and Mike McCaskey had served our country with distinction, earning their Purple Hearts in concert. One-time foxhole buddies, now my father was in a retirement community in another state, and McCaskey was working for me. As far as I knew, they hadn't spoken for thirty years.

And all the Purple Hearts in the world didn't seem to matter to either of them now.

As we pulled into the parking lot of Riverside, I pushed my maudlin thoughts aside and turned to look at Gino.

"I guess I just need to know that I can live this life alone and be happy. Thrive and not just survive, even if it means I go it alone for the rest of the journey. And what about Sam? Shouldn't I make sure I can handle the whole motherhood thing solo before adding a man to the equation? Having Nick front and center just muddies the waters for me right now. Keeps me believing the fantasy that I need someone else to make me complete—that focusing on Nick is enough to keep me happy. And it's not, G." I looked down at my hands. My voice had grown quiet.

"That is a good thing, m'hija. A very good thing. For only God can take that rightful place on the throne of your life, and He will not give it to another. Not even one as handsome as our Nick. Perhaps God is calling you to give Nick and your marital status over to Him, to lay them both like a sacrifice at the foot of the cross. *Amada*, God is bigger than your divorce." Gino's voice was strong, rich, Columbian, full-bodied coffee after a month of freeze-dried decaf.

The audio screen on the console lit up with three life changing letters: SAM. Gino's Bluetooth automatically connected with my phone whenever we were in his truck. Another advantage of having a techno-geek for a friend.

I pressed the button to accept her call.

"Hello, darling girl!" Joy warmed my voice.

"Josie! I miss you! Where are you?" Samantha's girlish trilling rang throughout the car.

Gino turned to me and smiled. I nodded.

"Como estas tu? Un abrazo fuerte de Tio Gino para ti, Carina."

"Tio Gino! When are you coming to see me?" Sam's excitement warmed my soul. I winced at her question.

"Very soon, *bonita*. And I will have a little *regalo* for you."

"I love you, Sam. And I can't wait to see you again … very soon. Uncle G and I are in the middle of a big investigation. When it's over, we'll both come and give you the biggest hugs ever." I kept my tone upbeat.

"And a regalo?"

"Sí, bonita!" Gino reached over and gave my hand a squeeze.

"When?" A hint of a whine from the bravest little girl I knew.

"Soon, sweetheart. Soon." My fingers caressed the volume button.

"Okay. Gotta go! I love you, Tio! I love you, Josie! Bye!" Sam ended the call, breathless and happy sounding.

Gino glanced at me. "You two are perfection itself together. You know this, *verdad*?"

"I do. It's just, I worry all the time. I love her, and I can't wait to have her in my life—in my arms, in my home—full-time. But I'm scared to death. And I don't even know what to do with Nick in the midst of all of this. Does he even want to be a father? Will having him around while I sort out my own crazy feelings just confuse her? I don't know, G." I shook my head, trying to get in front of the pressure building behind my temples. A remnant of yesterday's migraine? I hoped not.

"What we do know, m'hija, is that God has placed both Samantha and Nick in your life for a reason, and He is bigger than your fears."

"Here's hoping He's also bigger than this psycho. Let's go in there and figure out where she's taken Angela Murray." I opened my door and was about to spin out of the seat when Gino's paw found my shoulder.

"Let us do more than hope." Gino took my hand in his, closed his eyes, and bowed his head. "Heavenly Father, we come before Thee, begging Thy divine intervention as we come to this place in Thy holy name to do Thy work. We love Thee, *Dios todo poderoso*. And we pray that Thy love would cover Miss Angela as we seek her. Please protect her from the power of the evil one who has snatched her away from here, and give us wisdom and direction that we might find her before it's too late. Amen." He squeezed my hand and then dropped it.

I stepped out of the truck and into the pathway leading to the front entrance. Gino hesitated in the parking lot. "What's up, G? What are you looking at?"

"Is this not the place she would park?" He was staring at a blue and white sign reading "Director" and the blue sedan parked in front of it. "And is this not her car? Perhaps we should learn how long the car has been here. There are exterior cameras." Gino pointed to the gutters.

Small bubble cameras were mounted at consistent intervals along the roofline. Could it be that simple? *No way.* They couldn't have been operational when the killer had come for Angela. That would be too easy.

CHAPTER THIRTY-SIX

Saturday, March 26

"How would any killer smart enough to administer scopolamine be dumb enough to be caught on video abducting one of the victims?" Gino had unshakable faith, but this was a little much.

He concluded his roofline examination and joined me at the entrance. "Perhaps it is not about the desire not to be seen but rather the opposite."

"As in, she's taunting us again?" *Just like in the photos.* We pushed through the double sets of doors and turned left into the assisted living part of the facility. Two polyester-clad nurse's assistants tended to residents. A third woman, in loose blue pants and a V-neck, cartoon-splashed top, pushed Arnie down the hall.

"Perhaps." Gino stepped into the cafeteria and took over Arnie's chair, steering into dining position.

He locked the wheels and bent down low to talk to him. The man's head swiveled to look at Gino. His eyes were quite clear today, opening a window into the valiant, soft-hearted warrior he'd once been. The picture on his door featured a pixie-eyed blonde in a yellow sun dress looking up at her handsome man in uniform. Cuban phrases popped up out of their murmurings every few words. *Maybe Gino'll get something out of him.*

Ceci walked in my direction from the station down the hall. When our eyes met, she looked down at the threadbare floor.

"Good afternoon, Ceci." I smiled and walked past her.

She murmured a response, but I was already at the station. Two TV monitors were mounted behind the desk, in full view. One recorded inside shots, and one seemed to display nothing but outside shots. *Please be recording and not just displaying.* It was disheartening how many times people installed security equipment just for show. Why hadn't I thought about this system before? I hadn't needed to. I'd thought this place was safe.

Safe. Is anything, anyone, any place, safe anymore?

I stepped back out into the hall toward the cafeteria. Gino was seated next to Arnie, drinking what was probably lukewarm, watery coffee. With generic non-dairy creamer. God bless him. Everyone knew he'd rather drink weed killer.

"And now our lovely chief approaches. Could it be she wishes to dance with one of us?" He gave Arnie a light, conspiratorial elbowing. A slow, half-grin etched itself across Gino's face as he put his arm around Arnie's back, then rose to his feet. "Alas, *companero mio*, I fear it is me she seeks. Like the black widow spider stalking her prey."

"Relax, G. If I was stalking you, you'd be the last to know." I bent down and landed a kiss on Arnie's cheek. "I'll be back to walk you to your room after snack time." I waited for his slight nod before following Gino's receding figure down the hall.

If anyone could reveal the mysteries captured on tape by outdated security cameras, it was Gino.

Gino stopped at the empty nurse's station, looking around as if to assure himself that all staff and residents truly were otherwise occupied for the moment. He glanced down the hall a final time and then swung behind the laminate divider and started messing with dials and switches on a panel in front of the monitors. Within seconds, he had the footage moving forward and back with ease.

"We shall soon learn how lucky we are or are not today." He squatted in front of the panel.

"Looks like I've got a little time to kill." I wandered toward my mother's room. She rarely went to afternoon snack time, opting instead for her tray to be delivered. It would be better for her to get out more, but it would also be better for me to visit more often and take her out more. I sighed. At least she could afford a facility with tray service. *Tradeoffs*.

Her door was closed, as usual. I pulled the handle down and entered her little apartment. Her oxygen machine whooshed and hummed, but she wasn't in the kitchenette or living area. The plastic tubing lead from the oxygen unit into her bedroom. I peaked in. She was sound asleep. I stood over her bed for several seconds, staring at her bruises and offering up fervent prayers for safe-keeping and protection.

My cell phone buzzed with a text from Gino.

VENGATE. AHORITA.

Get over here. Now. I tucked a stray hair behind my mother's ear and left her sleeping. Then, I hurried to join Gino down the hall.

"*Mira.* Just take a look at this." Gino was on fire. Something big was up. He was wearing a rarely-seen pair of glasses. He'd managed to find a way to display a time and date stamp for the video feed from the various security cameras located inside and outside the facility. He finished rewinding one of the tapes and turned to look at me.

"Whaddya got?" Electricity flowed up and down my spine.

He stared at me without speaking.

"What did you find?" My heartbeat thundered in both ears, and my face burned. "G, what do you have?"

"It is more of a *who* than a *what*, m'hija. Quite the who indeed." He let out a deep breath and hit the play button.

The first clip showed footage of the parking lot. Leaves blowing, trees sagging, a very windy day. Gino's arms were folded across his chest. I mirrored him.

"Watch this next series very carefully." He hit a button to slow things down a notch. For several seconds, nothing showed on the screen but the occasional piece of paper flying through the parking lot and tree branches swaying in the wind.

Then a dark blue sedan pulled into the director's parking spot. The driver's door opened, and one boot-clad leg snaked out the door. And then Kira Stoklavich slid out, elegantly dressed, complete with dark glasses and a navy silk scarf wrapped around her head, Joanne Woodward style.

She walked toward the building, stopping several paces from the edge of the sidewalk, perfectly framed in the shot. She turned her face up to the camera, offered a little wave, and mouthed, "Catch me if you can."

CHAPTER THIRTY-SEVEN

Saturday, March 25

I kept staring at Kira's face on the screen after the clip ended. "What the heck?" Kira? Kira? "Is this some kind of joke? Or is this really possible, G?"

He took off his glasses, rubbed his eyes, and shook his head. "It can mean nothing else. And the fact that she is no longer hiding her identity and has led us here may mean that she intends to kill Director Murray and disappear for good … or end herself as well."

I shook my head. "But that makes no sense. Why go to all that trouble to frame me if she was just going to walk away from it all? What's her end game? To tease us, keep us on a string, only to disappear? I don't get it. And I'm pretty sure I don't believe it." I rubbed my temples. The string of violent deaths, starting with Del and leading us to Angela Murray. "Do you think we interrupted her, maybe ruined her timing somehow? This can't be the script she intended to play out all along. It doesn't make sense."

Gino kept fast-forwarding video clips next to me. I clenched my hand, tapped it on the desk top, opened it and spread my fingers wide. My legs were trembling. I sucked in air, forced it back out, stretched out my neck, and shook my head. I want to run after her. Now. But where? Where would we even start to look for her? I whipped out my cell phone.

Nick answered on the first ring.

"Kira. It's Kira. And if it's not her, she's working in concert with someone who's as evil as she is." Oops. What about Nick's broken relationship history with her? Had there ever even been one? *Who knows*. We could sort through that later. "Put out a BOLO, and then I need you to call in one of your favors and get a court order allowing us into her case files. We need someone to look through everything she's worked on and documented since the murders, and fast. And … start with mine."

"Josie?" Nick wasn't following me.

"She's targeting me. She's framing me by going after people I've talked about during our sessions. Get into those files. Start reading. There's got to be something to point us in some reasonable direction. Nick, I need it to be you. I know it's an investigation, but ..." God only knew what I'd said during my hours of therapy in her office. I needed some cover.

"Of course, beautiful. I'll read it myself and do all I can to only extract what's essential to the investigation." Warm tones infused his voice.

"Um ... what about the stuff that isn't essential to the investigation, but is essential to *me*?" A bead of sweat broke out on my forehead. A court order would be written in such a way that she'd have to give up *all* of her files. Once a file was entered into police custody, all real control was lost. "Ugh. What's one more personal humiliation out of series of thousands in the past several weeks?" I let out a deep breath.

"It doesn't have to be humiliating."

"Maybe not for you. But it will be for me." He wasn't getting it. Again.

"Some files are a lot less complete than you'd expect." His voice grew cold. Was he suggesting he was willing to bury evidence to protect me? "Nick, don't ..." I let my voice plead my case with the words I couldn't form. What would happen if he tampered with evidence and got caught? A better woman would ask a better question. How can I be dancing with the idea of ruining this good man's career just to protect my self-image?

"Not all things are under your control, Jo." He hung up before I could tell him not to do it. Not to take that kind of bullet for me.

I took a deep breath and put my phone back in my pocket with trembling hands. *Why do I always say the wrong thing? What about 'Don't even think about stepping over the line for me'? Why hadn't I said that?*

Nick would be freaked out if he read any of my regrets about having chosen Del over him—and my darkest fears about whether or not I was worthy of a man like Nick. He was my gold standard. Would I ever be good enough for him? So I'd chosen Del instead. Nick wasn't the most flexible thinker when it came to man-woman stuff in general. He wasn't a big fan of hearing about hard feelings that he couldn't fix, let alone those of the distorted nature I'd risked sharing more than once with Kira before I knew about her history with him.

What would happen when he read my files? How much of my warped thinking and ruminations about him and our complicated friendship, about my secret fears and longings, had Kira written down?

CHAPTER THIRTY-EIGHT

Saturday, March 26

"These sessions of yours, they are the key to this *maldita*, aren't they?" Gino appraised me through narrow eyes. "She plays a game with you. You are the mouse—she is the cat. She has been batting you about for how long now?" He kept his arms folded, casual.

"I don't know, G. Four, five years? How many sessions is that? How long has she been up to this? Who else has she killed? How did she stay so far under the radar?" *How can she be that much smarter than the rest of us?* "Hiding in plain sight. But for that long? And why target me? Why now?" All the stories she must've heard over the years. *Why had mine been the ones to trigger her murderous spree?*

"But there is much about you that is unique." Gino hadn't moved a muscle.

"Like what? This crap job full of angry people and unsolved murders that keep piling up? Take a look around my life—personally or professionally. I ain't exactly living the dream over here. What do I have that she could possibly want? What have I ever done that could drive her to this?" I dragged a hand through my hair, pulling on the ends.

My pulse beat as if I were a frantic lion in the middle of a kill-or-be-killed spree. I clenched the edge of the desk to keep from running as fast as I could, gathering my mother in my arms and leading as many of these gentle elders as I could out of this place. The building itself loomed, oppressive and unsafe. Had Gino felt it too?

"Enough of this crooked thinking, m'hija. You have done nothing to fall into the sights of this matadora. Whoa!" Gino erupted. "Did you feel that?" He looked puzzled. The lights flickered off and on in rapid succession.

"What just happened?"

Nurse's aides popped into the hallway from the cafeteria thirty feet down the hall. Ceci made her way toward us. I met her in the middle of the corridor and put my hand on her arm. "Is everything okay?"

"It's fine. Just a friendly little bump in the road of the wonderful world of construction. We get a little brown-out action every coupla days. It's nothing." Her words were measured.

"It was definitely something." *And the timing was awfully convenient.*

"We don't worry around here until we get the five and ten minute stretches. Our generators are excellent, but with as many special-needs residents and electricity-sucking machines as we have on this wing, like in your mother's room, we don't want to push our luck."

My mother's room? Was that a coincidence—or a threat?

Ceci turned and walked toward the cafeteria, and I returned to Gino.

Gino uncrossed his arms and hunched over the monitor. "You have that *I-don't-believe-it* look on your face, yet I tell you, it makes sense. All of this construction—this sort of thing happens with great frequency."

"So let's get back to Kira. Coming here. We need to get a tech crew on that car. Check out that still-shot again. Didn't she have gloves on when she got out of the car? I'm thinking she did. A la Audrey Hepburn."

"It was the director's car. That much is certain." Gino picked a picture up off of the desk featuring all the staff members posing in or around the car, parked in front of the "Director Parking" sign. Underneath the photo was the inscription, "We ♥ driving you crazy."

"If Kira did take Angela, why go to all the trouble of bringing it back here?" My head was spinning. There had to be psychopathological reasons for all of these careful steps of the dance. But what were they?

"It is part of the chase for her. The cat playing with her prey."

"So that makes us the prey. And the victims are just bait. She's using them to get to us."

"Not us, m'hija. You." He opened up a drawer in the nurse's station, started rifling through it.

"But why?"

"I am telling you, again—you have something the big cat wants. Badly." He pulled out a small flash drive, held it up, shook his head and replaced it.

"Badly enough to kill for." Something had to shake loose in my muddled brain.

"So it seems. You have the greatest meal of all in a heap at your feet for all the world to see, yet you refuse to eat." Gino's eyes hardened. "As is only right and just, but that is not how Kira would see it. She would see you as having the greatest quarry at your fingertips, and ignoring him."

"Nick …" A light ringing flitted through my left ear.

"Indeed."

"She's after Nick? But she had him." Icy shields wrapped themselves around my face.

"*Thought* she had him. Wanted to have him. But she lost out. To a far more beautiful hunter." Gino studied me. "And the most dangerous beauty of all …" His eyes squinted, released. "One that draws prey without intending, without even being aware of her powers of attraction. The kind a man like Nick cannot turn away from."

I stared at him. Stunned. "But, G, I … I never wanted—"

"Yes, as she so well knew. And your ambivalence, your woundedness, drew Nick to you like a moth to the flame. While she watched. And listened to excruciating details revealed during your sessions, no?" He shifted his weight, leaned a hip against the counter.

"Dear God, what have I set in motion?" Goose bumps rippled my flesh. A tremor shook my pocket. What was that? Then it happened a second time. Nick was calling me. He'd also left a text message:

PICK UP. STAT.

"Nick." My answer was a whisper. A harsh whisper.

"Are you still at Riverside?" Worry infused his voice.

"Yes. With G." Even though it wasn't one hundred percent fair, I was playing the part of Madame Butterfly, discovering her one true love's betrayal. And the sharp knife conveniently placed on her nightstand. *What happened between Kira and Nick? Who is he when he isn't with me? Should I have trusted him? Can I trust him moving forward?*

"I found something." His voice was flat.

"Me too." I was in junior high again. *Come on, Nick, go first.* But we didn't have that kind of time. We needed—I needed—to snap out of it. And catch a killer.

"I'm already on my way." He hung up before I could tell him what we'd found.

Why? Did he already know? "That was Nick. He's on his way over here."

"So I gathered. He has found something in the files. Something you may wish to tell me first, no? Something you might be feeling embarrassed by?" Gino turned to face me, leaning in. "What could be in those files to turn *la mala* against our Nick? If it is true that what you shared with her during your sessions became the roadmap to her victims, perhaps you will tell me what it is that you are so afraid of? What else might you have suggested about our good Saint Nicholas that may have incited her evil attention further?" Gino was all investigator now.

"I don't know. I don't remember everything. I just know I was a jumbled mess on more than one occasion. I mean, how many casual and professional conversations have I had with her over the past five years?" My chest tightened. Pain shot through my collarbone, down my right arm.

Is this what a heart attack feels like? What did I say about Nick?

My heart squeezed, hard. What happened between Nick and Kira, and how could I have missed it? Was Nick on Kira's side or mine? I glanced into a small round mirror tacked onto the wall. My ashen face stared back. A stranger to me.

Gino stepped forward and took me by the shoulders. "M'hija, there is no way our Nick is involved in any of this. *¿Me entiendes?* You must banish those lies and come back to the truth." He shook me ever so gently.

A single tear escaped my eye. Was he reading my mind? *Or am I that transparent?* Sludge filled my veins. "You don't know that, G. You can't know that. Who is anybody, really? How far can any of us ever really see into the heart of another?"

Nick. I was talking about Nick. But was he *my* Nick anymore?

CHAPTER THIRTY-NINE

Saturday, March 26

"Our Nick will be here in under five minutes. Let us invest our time in talking to the staff about the habits of the director." Gino picked up a legal pad and started writing.

I scrolled through my phone for messages. Mitch had left me three. *God bless her*. At least *she* was solid to the core. Wasn't she?

The first text contained all names and background information for every Riverside employee. I scrolled down the screen three times. The list kept going. I moved on to her second message. It contained a picture. I enlarged it as much as I could with my finger and thumb. Nick. On Kira's sofa. Time stamped and dated three days earlier. If that was even legit. The angle of the shot suggested Kira had taken it from her infamous captain's chair. Unless it'd be*en taken from a camera mounted over her desk.* A hidden camera? Why?

I turned a steely gaze on Gino. "Did you know about this? Can I trust *anybody* anymore?" Was everyone in my life a pseudo enemy?

His face walked from shock, to grief, to rage. He seemed to wrestle with the rage for a minute before putting it down. "You do not know what you are saying. I will forgive it. I forgive you these thoughts. It is all because of *la mala*. Her evil is all the more complete as she has worked among you, has gained your trust, the trust of the entire department, for years. And I tell you her betrayal—"

A loud blast thundered through the air. The wall behind Gino buckled and fell inward, plaster wallboard folding in half. Gino scrambled to his feet and rushed me, taking me down onto the hallway floor. My head smacked the thinly-padded concrete. A second blast erupted, and the trembling walls around us starting falling in.

My ears rang. Chalky dust filled the hallway. Ceiling tiles floated down around us. Beeps, hums, and alarms blared. Gino rose to his knees, shook his head. His lips moved, but no sound came out. Then he offered me his hand, pulled me up to a seated position. My head was light. I swallowed back vomit. I breathed in deep, filling my lungs with the hot, dirty air. Coughs savaged my throat.

A red and white calendar hung from one corner of what was left of the wall in front of me. The words were blurry, but I could make out a smiley face and the words "Happy B-Day Marian O." on one of the squares. *Mom? It has to be Marian Oliver!*

"Mom!" I shook my head and pushed to my hands and knees. I must hurry to my mother, to the twenty-seven other helpless men and women on the floor. "Call it in, G. I gotta go find my mother!"

As I fought to get to my feet, low moans from every direction broke through the smoke, like a giant hand turning up the volume on a low-rent sound system.

I pushed myself over to the edge of the hallway, eyeing the steel bars that used to hide behind sheetrock. I wrapped my hands around one and pulled myself to my feet. Dust rushed through the corridor on the back of a ferocious wind. To my right, the entire bank of windows behind the nurses' station had blown out. What had happened in my mother's room?

My right leg dragged behind as I limped down the debris-laden hallway toward room 1200. Tiny pieces of green glass crunched under my feet, the remains of a vase—its plastic tulips scattered. Shreds of paper unmoored from bulletin boards flew around like angry birds. The wind was distinct, layered over a hundred other noises.

I stopped for a moment. Low wattage lights lined the hallway floors and remaining exit signs—the blasts must've taken out the electricity. Every single resident on this wing depended on at least one device to keep them alive—how long could the generators keep my mother's oxygen machine operating?

I sniffed. Fire? *Or is this just how it smells when a bomb goes off?*

In the gloom of the hallway, only two rooms lay between me and the next exit sign. I tried to sprint, but pain shot through my right knee and climbed up my thigh. I reached up to wipe the sweat from my brow with the back of my hand. It came away sticky and red. A paneled door appeared through the dust on the right. Room 1202. Was someone trapped inside? I pushed through the door and glanced around the tiny studio. Empty. *Thank You, God.*

I lurched down the hallway to Mom's room. The door hung sideways, the top two sets of hinges dangling. I squeezed past it and tried to call out her name, but my mouth was a dry canyon. Thick waves of nausea rolled through me.

Cold wind ravaged the air in her little space like a dusty tomb. *Broken windows?* Her oxygen machine lay on its side, red line stuck at the fourth level, no telltale whooshing sound, no humming, dead. Could she breathe through the dust and pull in enough of the cool air winding its way through her apartment? Bedroom—she'd been in her bedroom. I pulled down on the claw handle and opened the door. My mother was on her side, trying to sit herself up in bed, wide eyed. I clung to the doorframe, bracing against a curtain of dizziness. Her forehead twinkled with glass. Tiny dots of blood formed a crown on her head. Her face was ashen. Our eyes met—she pushed her birdlike frame into a seated position and pointed a thin finger my way.

I made it to her side, tears dulling my eyes as I brushed the glass off of her pajamas and into my hand. I leaned in and reached my arms around her meager frame. Time to move her to safety. My right arm encircled another arm, strong and rough with rocky muscle. What? Nick was behind me, circling my mother and me with his arms. *Nick! Here? How could I have doubted this glorious man?*

He pressed his lips against my ear. "Can you stand up, beautiful?"

Was he whispering? Screaming? My ears were still buzzing. I nodded my head. "Take her out of here." My throat burned from the smoke. "*Get her out* now!"

He took off his leather jacket, wrapped it around her, and then folded her into his arms like a china doll. He held her in both arms, jutting an elbow out to me. I grabbed onto him with both hands and pulled myself to my feet. Waves of dizziness and nausea swept over me.

"Go! Through the windows!" I squawked at him, my throat raw.

I jabbed a thumb at what was left of the three floor-to-ceiling windows flanking my mother's bed. He picked through the broken glass like a panther, pausing in front of the window. Large hunks of glass hung low, quivering. We couldn't go through it without risking it falling on us.

Tension rifled up the arm I clung to. *No way, Nick. There's no turning back now*. Breaking away from him, I grabbed the comforter off my mother's bed, threw it over my shoulder, and hoisted myself toward the craggy window. The sprinkler system kicked on, spitting streams of tepid water over us.

I pushed my shoulder into the remaining shards of glass hanging like stadium pennants from the top of the window frame, breaking them off, clearing a path to safety. I motioned for him to take my mother through, but he stood stock still behind me.

I waited a few more seconds, but he still didn't move. I turned to match his gaze. *The opening I just cleared is too small for both of them.* I yanked the comforter up to cover my head and shoulders. Then I stretched out both arms, bunched my hands into fists, pulled them into my shirt sleeves as best I could, and barreled head-first through the glass, toward the fresh air of freedom. Just as another explosion threw me forward.

CHAPTER FORTY

Saturday, March 25

I awoke amidst a thick field of swamp grass sticking into my belly. My left boot was being pulled away from my body. My right foot was bare, cold, and pulsating with stabs from hot pokers. Orange and yellow starbursts painted the night sky. The air was ripe with fuel and blood and death. Nick. I turned my head toward a bloody body next to mine.

Nick!

"Josie!"

A spark of pain jolted my eyes open, pushing away the dark images.

"There you are, beautiful!" Nick loomed over me, handsome and very much alive. "Now that you're awake, I'm moving aside to let the paramedics have their way with you again." Nick's eyes reflected love and warmth and life.

I sat up, slapping at gloved hands as they tried to hold me down. Water was shooting onto the building from all directions. Flames licked out of second story windows. *Mom!* Where was my mom?

A cold blast of wind battered my face. I put my hands on the shoulders of the man in front of me and pushed myself to my feet. Nick must've paved the way. The paramedic didn't try to stop me. An ambulance idled behind me. Two men bent over a stretcher, speaking in low tones to my mother. They'd already dabbed away the bloody crown. She was nodding feebly—in good hands. What about the others?

"Gino—where's Gino?" I willed one uncooperative foot in front of the other. But neither one obeyed.

Nick wrapped his arms around me, murmuring into my ear. "He's alright—he made it out the cafeteria doors, with two residents the first trip. Then he made it back in and out for more residents twice before the first engine arrived. He's fine."

My breath struggled past the tightness in my chest. "We gotta get back in there." What about Arnie's wistful face as he lay prostrate on the thinning carpet? "Arnie! Did he get out? Did you see him?"

"He's out. They're all out. By the grace of God, none of the residents were injured in the fire." He rattled this out authoritatively.

"You can't know that. The building's just being evacuated." Well, that might not be true. Had I passed out? Nick responded with a long stare.

"How long have I been laying here?"

"About fifteen minutes. Long enough for the paramedics to clean you up and make sure your bumps, bruises, and burns are only skin deep. But, given how long you were out, you may have a concussion."

"Well, that's a relief. *For me*." It came out a whisper that should have sounded stronger—more confident, with a little swagger. But an invisible knife had creased my stomach lining. *Is my mother going to make it? What about the others?*

Nick pushed my bangs out of my eyes with one hand. "It's okay, Josie—everybody got out. Your mother's fine."

"How many explosives?"

"Three that we know of so far. Jibes with Gino's description of your hallway interlude. And the timing was almost flawless." He pulled me several feet away from the ambulance, giving us some makeshift privacy.

I cocked an eyebrow at him. "What do you mean?"

"Awfully convenient explosion—that's what I'm saying." He leaned against a young pine tree on the lawn, pulling me into his chest.

I trembled as our bodies touched, then inched away. Public displays of affection, when I didn't know what I wanted between us and couldn't remember what had just happened, were not on the menu right now. I pulled his arm out from around me. "What are you trying to say?"

The annoyed look in his eyes melted into resignation. He shifted on his feet, maintaining eye contact. "Josie, it took about fifteen minutes to evacuate the building just now. And, that doesn't take into account any time lost when we were working on getting your mother to safety."

Is Nick getting all paternalistic over me knocking out the window? I shook my head, filing that away for later. "Enough about my daring escape strategies. Where's Kira?"

CHAPTER FORTY-ONE

Saturday, March 26

Nick smiled and traced a finger over my cheek. "Welcome back, Chief."

"Forget me for now. Where's Kira? Where's Angela Murray?" Was she still alive? Too many mysteries.

"We have four teams out scouring the surrounding areas while we continue to work the case from here. But we did answer one question." He was calm, watching the comings and goings of the emergency crew.

"And?" Where was this going? Kind of like me and Nick.

"And Kira thought she could pick us all off with one big bang. A trifecta, of sorts." Anger laced his words. "She set us up—arranged it so we'd all be in the same place. She lured us here—like mice. She held the wedge of cheese and watched us dance at the pull of her strings."

"But how could she know we'd all be here at the same time?" I blinked back some lightheadedness. I had to stay in the game. "The photos? From this morning?"

"She had to know that would be good enough to lure at least two of us out here. Probably even knows us well enough to predict that it would be you and Gino. Knows you well enough to expect that you'd want her files searched. Personally. Confidentially." His eyes bored into mine.

"And that I'd send you to do it. And that you'd find something in them." She was that calculating.

"Written to send me straight back to you." The anger crept back into his voice. *Directed at Kira... or me?* "I got here just before the explosion." He flicked his eyes down. My eyes followed his to his bandaged hand.

"Wait, *before* the explosion?"

"Yes. I told you that. The explosion happened less than five minutes after I entered the assisted living wing to find you. We need to talk." His voice was welcoming, but not the look in his eyes.

What did he find in those files? My gut was a cold fist. "Okay, but not now. We have to make sure everyone is accounted for, and then we've got to get back into what's left of the director's office and look for anything that can tell us where Kira might have taken her."

I'd sat on Kira's overstuffed couch, session after session, whining like a school girl. Sharing all of the unthinkable secrets that lodge themselves inside the nooks and crannies of the human heart. No doubt, lots of it was ugly, unflattering, vulgar even. But what had I said that would rattle Nick enough to get him here that fast?

I'd said things about Nick that no man would want to hear or read. But he'd been around the water cooler enough times to know that was SOP when dealing with women. Most women. *And now he knows it applies to me, too. So what?* That couldn't be it. Could it? Only one way to find out.

"Nick?" I didn't have to fake the puzzled voice.

He stared at me, in silence, his kind eyes brimming with tenderness. *He's so perfect. Why can't I just let him love me? Why am I so afraid?* Gino trudged toward us, a smoky silhouette against the glowing building. I ran up to him and almost toppled him with my hug.

He was a dark gray mass of sludge and soot. There was a broad, jagged gash on his forehead. Paramedics appeared, as if summoned, but Gino waved them away.

"You were already my hero, G. How many did you save?"

He shook his head, closing his arms tighter around my quivering frame. "They are the heroes of the greatest generation. They saved me, m'hija. And I would walk through fire for them again." The whispered words sank deep within me. I stored them away to pull out and dissect with him in the weeks ahead.

"Nick's got something." I pulled away from him, nodding at Nick.

Gino turned, keeping one arm solidly around my waist.

"She'd written what had to be an imaginary quote from an imaginary conversation. But it was spot on. Definitely you. Even though it wasn't. And when I got here … it was almost too late." Nick pinched a fold of skin between his eyebrows.

"What was the quote?" I was throwing him a lifeline, ignoring the open Kira-and-Nick door. For now.

He sighed, dropping blank shields down over his eyes. "She'd written lots of drivel, interspersed with what could be legit—it was hard to tell.

Then she'd dive into your supposed psyche, typical mother-daughter, love-hate kind of stuff. But when I read your alleged raging statements about me and what could have been Kira, I knew it had to be a set up. And my next step was to your side."

He was like a lighthouse, head rolling to fix his gaze on Gino, scanning me, and back to Gino again.

Gino linked arms with me. He shifted his weight from one foot to the other, chuffing in thought. "And you knew she was here, so you flew into the trap. Like a cat to the catnip."

"From one hot mess to another." *Hmmm. That reminds me of something.* And then it was gone. "But you still haven't shared the mystery quote." He was getting weirder and weirder.

"I'm not sure it matters." He scuffed his heel on the ground. "But for what it's worth, you were talking about feeling like a victim."

"Of what?" I furrowed my brows.

"'You are a victim of the rules you live by.' Does that phrase mean anything to you?" Nick searched my face. "What's your number one rule?"

"Rule?" I gave him a blank stare. "You lost me at 'victim,' and this isn't making anything clearer."

"One of the golden rules: 'Honor thy father and thy mother.' Ring any bells?" He stepped closer to me, prompting Gino's arm to tighten around my arm.

"'Honor thy father and thy mother.' That's it? That's the big clue? You know my father's been so far out of my life it isn't even worth talking about, and my mother ..." I cast a glance over to where the ambulance carrying my wounded mother had been moments ago.

"You honor your mother, m'hija. To know you is to know this about you. To hear this is to know it means this place, where you honor your mother. But it is not to know who said this thing, you or la mala, and if indeed it was la mala, then I am inclined to Nick's point of view." Gino unlinked his arm from mine. He needed his other hand to emphasize his point. "This, this was part of her design from the very beginning."

I soaked it in for a moment. The complexity of it, the weight of it, the sheer evil of Kira's planning oozed in like concrete all around me, sucking me under, waiting to seal me in.

CHAPTER FORTY-TWO

Saturday, March 26

"But if she planted the evidence to lure us all here before she took Angela, how would she have known when to detonate the explosives?" I put my jangled nerves aside, unleashing the cop within.

"What does it mean—Wait. Cameras?" Nick looked up at the remaining light poles and nearby trees, scanning for surveillance equipment.

Maybe. "What if it was simpler than that? What if she somehow managed a line of sight?" I paused. "She'd want to watch, right? The whole cat and mouse thing—she'd want to watch. And if that's the case, then her hidey-hole can't be that far away."

"And if there is any chance that Miss Murray is still alive ..." Gino picked up my trail. "She'd be in that killer's lair, facing la mala, perhaps right now. If only we knew *where* ..."

"No. Not right now. Right now, Kira's watching us. She'd have to. It'd be too much fun for her to miss." I spun around, searching the bluffs jutting up behind the cornfields. "She's out there somewhere. In a cave, in a mound, in a deer blind. She's not that far away from us. She can't be."

Nick had been texting furiously while we talked. I opened my hands wide, stretched my fingers, closed them again. "Please tell me that whatever you're ordering up over there includes a couple of canine teams."

"And the cavalry. And a few of my own best hunters. I got a guy or two loves this kind of thing." He didn't look up from his phone.

"The actual cavalry, or is that some sort of nickname? If you're talking about the Hoof Beat Club, they're not going to be able to do much more than kick up some noise. They're pretty much just a volunteer horse club with shotguns."

"And you no doubt went to high school or horse camp or something with half of them." He finished texting and looked up at me, amusement dancing in his chocolate brown eyes.

"I may know one or two of them." I'd ridden either rodeo or competitive trail rides with most of them at some point in my life. "And I know they're all solid riders and pretty good shots. But if Kira feels cornered, she'll shoot her way out. She has everything to lose now, and I don't want any of them getting hurt. I don't want any of them coming up against her. It's not worth it."

"They won't be. They won't ever get close enough. Think of them as decoys. Trotting catnip to pull Kira's eyes away from us long enough for us to get a bead on her, keep her on the run. Anything to keep her from getting up close and personal with Angela."

"But for how long?" Even though my horse buddies volunteered to help protect and serve, they hadn't volunteered to be bait.

Gino stepped up and pulled a rectangular box from his back pocket. "Long enough for us to catch the big cat. This little *reloj* may be of some use." Gino opened the box and picked up what looked like a watch, holding it up for us to see.

"Go on. What's it do?" Gino wasn't a watch guy. This had to be one of his high-tech security gadgets.

Nick studied the device. "That a GTL?"

"It is." Gino's eyes sparkled.

Nick let out a low whistle. "I thought it wasn't out yet, something not quite right with the trials?"

"Technology and politics do not mix. That is what we have learned from the hold ups in Springfield and Washington. It does not stop us from experimenting in the meantime." Gino fidgeted with the thing, twisting small dials, holding it up to face the bluffs, fidgeting again.

Nick signaled for a few of his men to come forward. Two large men in dark khaki jumpsuits emblazoned with FBI on the back stepped up. "You'll like these two, Gino. Straight off the line from the computer crimes boot camp in Virginia."

Gino's eyes lit up, and he crooked a finger, inviting the agents to lean in before explaining the nuances of his latest toy.

Nick moved close enough to touch me, but didn't. "There were quite a few other clues that were pretty telling in Kira's notes. Lots of things I don't think you'll want to read yourself, let alone submit officially for the investigation." He crossed his arms, brushing my side with his elbow.

I stiffened. Any one of a dozen unpleasant themes from my sessions with Kira could be involved here. Had she targeted her victims after people we'd talked about? Who else had we talked about? Sam! Was my little girl safe from her?

"Nick! I've got to check on Sam. What if that psycho goes after my girl!"

Nick pulled out his cell and offered it to me. "Call her, beautiful. We'll take five, and I'll get a team assigned to her while you're checking in."

I pulled my own phone out of my pocket and dialed her number, but she didn't pick up. A second later, a text came through.

Can't talk now. Luv u! Cu later?

The tightness in my shoulders fell away. I answered her.

Love you more! See you soon. Call you later. Love, love, love you!

Thank you, Mighty God. Please protect her. And bring me back, bring all of us back, to love this little girl and raise her up right.

What else might be in Kira's files? This was my chance to steer Nick away from sacrificing himself by 'cleansing' the files in a valiant attempt to safeguard my integrity in front of my men. "It's too soon to say what will be important from Kira's files and what won't be necessary. I have no way to gauge that now. Not without taking a look myself. Not without getting Kira behind bars. And we won't have time for the one until we do the other." *Not my most eloquent speech, but I think I made my point.*

"I'm less worried with how intact the files remain than how intact the woman I love remains." He put his hand on my arm, turning me to meet his eyes. Unfettered love swam there. What would he find in mine?

"Nick …" I had no way to finish that sentence. This was not the time or place to have this talk. Again.

"There's a new thread in her notes that I didn't know about. If it's even true." He coughed and looked at the ground.

"Why do I think this is going to be another bit of news I'm not going to like?" My guts clenched.

Nick took a deep breath and closed his eyes. "Kira says in her notes that you were convinced that Del had been sleeping with lots of women. That you even wondered out loud about her and Del … She suggests you were obsessed with it, couldn't shake it, and it was powerful enough to drive you to irrational behavior. Maybe even violence. But that's not all. I found audio files. With the initials D.R on at least one of them. As in 'Del Reed,' maybe?"

"What?"

I moved over to lean against the tree, Nick following me. Gino and the men gestured toward one set of bluffs, voices muffled.

"It does kind of make sense, in terms of the perfect frame up. Luring Del into some sort of weird relationship, taping it, and then using it to tighten the noose she'd worked so hard to tie around your neck." Nick stood alongside me, our bodies touching, his warmth shielding me from another round of frigid breezes.

If you thought about the evidence like a killer would, it did make some sense. Pretty low-hanging fruit. Especially if she had been sleeping with Del. Which wasn't the point. "Is there anyone I care about she *hasn't* slept with?"

The muscles in Nick's jaw tightened. He kept his gaze on the horizon. "There was more in the notes. A lot more. Most of it had a staged quality about it, but there were threads of you in almost every case she worked on. She was obsessed."

I frowned. "What do you mean, *'threads of me'*?"

He shifted his weight to the other leg, and his hip pulled away from mine. "It almost didn't matter who she was counseling. Her notes had a common denominator in them—you. You were referenced in the dirty cop's files. But not from Schlichting—that wouldn't have bothered me. She made separate notations in her files wondering how his actions would make you feel. I had to work a little to find them, but they were there, password protected and filed under 'Miscellaneous J.'"

"But why me?" Fog circled my brain.

"That one we may never fully understand. But a quick walk through her notes makes it clear that you were, are, and have probably always been, her main target. And this is just the tip of the iceberg. I only combed through your files, Del's files, Deter's files, and Schlichting's files. And found enough data in all of them to paint a killer picture. She had it out for you. Wanted to be you maybe? Take what you had? Punish you? I don't know. I just know it's all there."

"Which is another thing that makes no sense. Why would she leave so much evidence? Why incriminate herself?"

"The psychopath in her, maybe? I don't think she ever dreamed anyone could come this close. And she must've thought today's ruse was good enough to take the three of us out with one big boom." Nick's ruminations were interrupted by the flushed appearance of Gino and the two field agents.

They'd found something.

CHAPTER FORTY-THREE

Saturday. March 26

"Several possibilities have emerged. We're using a series of satellite heat sensors as simple tracking devices." Gino was breathless. "Field teams are on their way to each location indicated on our monitors now. We're running a program designed to track any heat signature fitting the basic footprint of a living creature over one hundred pounds. Once the mass requirements have been met, a simple body-type recognition program eliminates any non-human forms. And if we pinpoint any remaining heat signatures, it looks something like this."

Gino held up a handful of topographic maps. "Teams have been dispatched to every site but the two closest to where we are standing right now."

"Which one rings your internal alarm the loudest?" Nick's voice was steely.

Gino help up his 'watch,' as if we could see what he knew was there. "Given the location of the heat stamps, this one big black dot makes the most sense to me. And given that our lovely chief knows this area perhaps better than we do, I am thinking she could best verify which of the two locations we would wish to attend to personally." Gino floated next to me, hand outstretched to give me a good view of his glowing doo-dad.

"And?" Nick stepped alongside Gino and me, staring at the GTL.

"The first two dots represent a gas station and a farmhouse. But the strongest heat stamp radiates from a point about half a mile that way." Gino pointed his finger to the largest arrow on the dial, then extended it dramatically in the general direction of the eastern bluff. "So tell us, Josie, what would be out in that thick spot of woods? Are you not a member of the hunting club with rights to this land?"

"I certainly am. Whitney's Basin. And within Whitney's Basin, there are three well-known deer blinds. But one is a bit bigger than the others. It'd make a great hideout. The occasional hunter coming and going on these bluffs wouldn't raise suspicion this time of year. Hunters have been known to scout the area, watching the herds, counting does and fawns, searching for mushrooms maybe. Of course, coyotes are a popular target too. And a confident woman tramping through these woods at odd hours, wearing the right clothes and toting hunting gear around, wouldn't be questioned."

But how would she get her victims there? Did she have help? Had she literally gone hunting with Angela?

"And it's not unusual for hunters to roam the woods in pairs. Nobody would be bothered by her bringing people hither and yon." Gino was tracking with me, scanning the bluffs.

"Bonus that it's so close to Riverside ... and to my mother." The creep factor sent shivers up and down my spine. "How long has she been planning this killing spree?"

"A lot longer than the string of vics from Del to Murray." Nick was scrolling through his cell phone. "I took pictures of a few of the more disturbing client case files when I was doing my quick review. Listen to this excerpt, from nearly a year ago." He turned the phone sideways and started to read. "The chief presented in an agitated state, perseverating on the lack of justice in the juvenile system. Particularly upset over the abuse suffered by a foster child at the hands of her own parents prior to her being removed from their custody. Wishing they were dead—saying she'd like to kill them with her own hands. Her barely controlled anger troubles me greatly." Nick's voice trailed away into silence.

Gino turned away from the bluffs to look at me. "*¡Maldita!* That one is nothing but an evil witch! How she has gained and exploited your confidence in every way will never be forgotten." Crimson flooded his cheeks, and the GLT trembled in his grasp.

"So, Sam's parents—as I recall, there was an accident, verdad? Did they not burn to death? A very unpleasant way to go. So perhaps what looked, at the time, like another faulty wiring system in an old two flat in a poor neighborhood was much more than met the eye. Was really arson. La mala—it seems she likes to play with fire."

I'd felt no sorrow for them at the time, given the allegations of horrific child abuse I'd received unofficially from William, Sam's case worker.

But in the months after the fire, my life was forever changed as my heart wrapped itself around Samantha and fueled a new destiny—motherhood. Without the fire, there'd have been no Sam in my life.

"So, if Kira has killed so many, she has burned alive, what else has she done? How long, and in how many other places has she hunted before?" Gino pulled the unthinkable out into the light.

"She was part of the county infrastructure before my time." I crossed my arms, counting back. "And it's been what, almost five years for me?"

"If memory serves, back then she was still teaching at the university part time. Which would make it her sixth year here." Nick added.

He would know, right? *Stop.* I couldn't go there. I'd been married at the time. And Kira was an attractive, single, professional barracuda of a woman. Just the way Nick liked them. But who had tracked who in that trade? Had she known even then how much Nick and I meant to each other? Was that why she'd chosen him? Or did her obsession with Nick lead her to me—her competition?

Which came first, the me-obsession or the Nick-attraction? "So, you're thinking that would've been an excellent pool for new prey?"

"On it." Nick looked up and stepped over to one of the FBI-emblazoned men milling around. He gestured to an SUV beside the agent, and they both got in.

I shook my head and faced Gino. "More rabbit trails. Just what we don't need. We just need to find Kira and Angela. So, back to Whitney's Basin. I think we go directly to the tricked-out blind and see what we can see. My money's on that being her home away from home." I turned to follow the black SUV as it threaded its way toward us.

Nick was at the wheel, with the dark-clad agent riding shotgun. He rolled to a stop in front of us. Gino opened one of the back doors and held it for me. I slid in behind Nick and whispered into his ear, "I got a bad feeling about this. What if we find something neither one of us want to face? Are you ready for that?"

Nick froze for a few seconds. Had he heard me? Then he turned around to look at me, held his hands out to me. When I offered him my hand, he wrapped both of his around mine and held on tight for several seconds before responding. "I'm ready to face anything with you, Jo."

Nick gave my hands a final squeeze and released them. Then he steered the SUV out of the cluttered parking lot, turning right out of the complex. He looked at me in the rear view mirror. "What's the fastest route?"

"Stay on Mine Road till you hit the stop sign. Then make a right and follow 123 for a couple miles. The park entrance will come up on the right, but it takes you to the camp sites. Pass it, and go another mile until you see an unmarked asphalt service road on your right, and take it." I shifted my attention to the other agent. I touched him on the shoulder and stuck my hand out. "Chief Jo Oliver. Thanks for joining us on this death ride."

"Jack Hathoway. Known your buddy Nick for longer than I'd like." The agent's grip was firm. We all laughed and exchanged nods.

The SUV bounced along the highway toward Whitney's Basin. Nick and Gino spoke in hushed tones, planning what to do first, second, and third. Hathoway was monitoring other field agents as, one by one, the teams checked in.

"Clear," was all they said. They hadn't found her yet.

We crested a hill. The late afternoon sun was a gray ball streaked over by dark clouds. Trees littered the horizon, broken by a swath of asphalt streaming like a velvety ribbon adorning an emerald river.

Just like when, a million years ago, my dad had driven an old red International pickup truck with a hard plastic steering wheel and a worn clutch. A seatbelt pinched my hips as I sang ancient spirituals in a low voice. Dad was smiling, tapping along with a thumb on the wheel, cigarette held between curling lips. I sat on two pillows so I could see over the dash as we drove through the night. I loved to watch signs of the night—bright eyes darting along the roadside, fireflies lighting up the trees like Christmas lights.

Without warning, a buck bounded up out of the ditch, leaping over a culvert and into the road in front of us. My dad's right arm sprang out, holding me against the seat back as he slammed on the brakes. We skidded to a stop, the buck frozen in place. Bright lights showcased him perfectly. Majestic figure, magnificent rack. One foot up, as if questioning whether to go forward or back. His brown eyes stared straight into mine. And for the first time ever, I fell in love.

My dad let his arm fall from its protective position. "Look, kid. He's a beauty. And he's looking right at you. Must've been listening to you sing."

My six-year-old self marveled at the possibility.

"Really, Dad?" My voice squeaked with excitement.

"Really, kid. Animals hear us. They sense all kinds of things about us. They can tell a good man a mile away. Better 'n us that way."

The glorious animal placed its hoof back on the pavement, faced the east bluff, and started to meander off the road. He stopped, turned back, and looked at me again. My little girl self-morphed into me, watching him as he gave his impressive antlers a shake toward the narrow opening in the tree bank off the corner of the woods he was facing.

"Stop here."

Nick threw me a confused look, but pulled the SUV off to the shoulder of the road.

I opened my door and sprang out. There … a break in the tree line at the far corner of the bluff. "There. We start there."

Nick and Gino followed me in silence.

"What the …?"

I turned. Hathoway stood on the pavement, in front of the SUV's hood, roughly where the buck had been in my vision.

"Rule number one—Don't question a country girl. Especially not in the woods." I winked at him and continued my trek to the bluff, all three men trailing behind me.

CHAPTER FORTY-FOUR

Saturday, March 26

I stopped ten yards away. It was a typical home-made deer blind—weathered pine board sitting atop a sturdy old oak. Wooden steps nailed into the massive trunk. But reddish brown splotches trailed down the tree, streaking the boards. Something about it said it was recently abandoned. We wouldn't find Kira here, but we might find something. Someone. I closed my eyes.

God, please. I need You. I need Your supernatural strength. I need Your courage.

Hathoway searched the perimeter, alternately bending down and looking up. Checking for explosives? Tripwires? Smart man.

Gino and Nick stood together on the other side of the blind, facing me. Nick nodded at Gino, and he pulled the box from his pocket once again. What else could it do?

Gino's expression went from hopeful to frustrated as he scanned the scene with his latest toy. Whatever he was searching for wasn't here. He broke the silence. "It is of no use. She is gone."

Gino put the box back into his coat pocket and stepped into the clearing.

I'd seen him use a fancy gadget that could tell a live body from a dead one. Made sense he'd fuse one technology onto another.

"There are only four live heat marks in this radius." He kept his voice lowered.

Respecting the dead? *Please, God. Keep the courage coming.* "But more than four bodies?"

His other contraption could detect shapes, sizes. Sort of like a Lowrance fish finder, but for the Earth and her woodland creatures. *Fish finders, deer finders, where's the sport in all that?*

He nodded.

Nick was at my side a fraction ahead of Gino. Nick touched my arm as I clicked the safety back on and holstered my Glock. He looked up at the blind, at the six two-by-twos leading up to it. "I'm going up."

He put a gloved hand on the lowest board.

I shook my head. "My county. My party." I put my hand over his. "Besides, you'll love the view from down below."

I winked.

He stepped aside, sank to one knee, and eyed me expectantly. Was he about to propose? He raised an eyebrow and patted his knee, offering me a boost. I smiled and placed one boot on his thigh, snapped some crime scene gloves on, and climbed up one ragged rung after another. I would probably have to slip on another pair of gloves by the time I reached the top.

Strong coppery air wafted down to me as I climbed closer to the mouth of the blind. It was closed on three sides, with a primitive roof, pitched enough to keep the snow and ice sliding off when the weather warmed up. Larger hands than mine had held these makeshift rungs over the generations. But smaller hands than mine had left one perfect bloody handprint on the top board.

I avoided the handprint. Finally, some real evidence. She had to be on the run so far and so fast she thought we'd never find her. Or decompensating. That happened, right? Killers came apart at the seams for no good reason? I kept my eyes trained on the bloody handprint. What horrible scene would I find inside the rickety blind?

"And?" Nick must've read my body language. Knew I'd found something.

"Handprint. Bloody. And small." I kept my head down, letting my eyes find his. "Not looking forward to this next bit. The smell's enough to knock a guy off a ladder." I blanched as the wind shifted.

"Good thing we sent up the girl." He lifted his chin, encouraging me to do what I had to do.

I nodded at him, breathing in deeply before straightening my head and facing the blind. The ceiling beams came in to view first, and I caught a glimpse of sky between the slats. I raised myself up on my toes and lifted one hand up to clutch the floor.

Resistance. My hand pushed against something thin and taut, stretched across the doorway. Too tough to be a spider web. What could it—

Trip wire!

Too late. My hand had pushed past it, breaking the wire. I gasped, frozen in place.

"Babe?" Nick's voice was a heavy load of worry.

I shook my head, alternately grabbing the wood step with one hand, and flexing the fingers of the other, taking inventory. I waited another several seconds to quell the shaking in my legs before responding. "Nothing. Fine. I'm fine. Definitely something here." My muscles quivered. Finish the climb? Or go back? *I'm here. I'm going in.*

I pushed my head up over the edge. Should have gone back. There was Angela Murray's body, hanging from a rope, gutted like a deer. Dark red sludge trailed down her legs. She was wearing a black Lone Ranger mask.

Bile rose in my throat. I could not, would not, puke all over the evidence. *Focus.* I pulled my eyes away from her. What was that? I took one step down the ladder. How long had it been since I'd touched the wire? Thirty seconds? Sixty? Nothing had happened. I shook my head and dropped my foot another step, descending the crude ladder. Retreating.

The trill of a bell stopped me. Just as I wondered if it had sounded only in my head, it rang again. Coming from the blind. I patted the lip of the blind and found the small rectangular shape, folding it into my gloved hand. I moved the phone down with one hand to the other, still clinging to the board for dear life. Then I used the tip of my gloved finger to hit the green button. I studied the symbols, found the little speaker button, punched it.

"Oliver." I knew who it would be.

"Josephine. I really hoped it would be you that answered my call. Still hanging in there? How do you like my little tableau?" *Present tense. Is she watching me right now?*

Tiny fangs pierced my temples. "What do you want?"

"Come on, Chief. Don't play dumb. It's beneath us both."

"You're a coward." White flashes of anger slowed my reaction times.

"Oh, now you're talking. Don't stop. Please." She paused, lowered her voice to a snarl. "How's it feel to fail? How do you like knowing I'll always be one step ahead of you? Knowing I'll strike again, happily taking out the trash you weren't woman enough to handle. You should be thanking me. How does it feel, knowing I'm better than you'll ever be?"

"You're not better than me. You're not anything. You're like a cat, playing with her food, batting around a dead mouse." Maybe she would make a mistake if I stooped to her level.

"Now you're just being a sore loser. What's wrong, Jo? Trail gone cold? All out of moves?" Amusement laced her voice. We could've been talking about a card game.

"*I'm* the loser? You're taunting me in the middle of the woods, at a safe distance. Why don't you heat it up a little? You won't though, will you? You're too much of a coward to give me a real clue. You don't like it hot, do you, Kira?" *Please take the bait. Come on, Kira, you think you're smarter than me? Prove it.*

"Oh, I like it plenty hot. No doubt about that. Just ask Nick."

Ouch. Should've seen that one coming.

CHAPTER FORTY-FIVE

Saturday, March 26

The line went dead. A river of ice gorged my veins, deadening my heart, and ravaging my lungs. The phone clunked out of my hand down the side of the tree, swooshing into the leaves below.

"*Just ask Nick.*" My Nick? Or hers?

The piercing darts of pain grew, burrowing deep into my forehead, drawing a tight band of steel around my head. Hot tears streaked down my face, and I clamped both eyes shut. Would I never find a man who wanted only me?

"But why, Nick?" Had I just said that out loud?

"Josie … Jo." Nick's soft voice rose to meet me. Was that pity in his tone?

I moaned, swaying into the wind, two hands clinging to the same board. Not exactly stable.

"No, beautiful. Don't let her do this to us. You know better." His voice was steady now. Growing stronger. Nearer.

His hand grazed my calf, his touch evoking more tears. I shook my head. "Go away, Nick. I'm coming down. Get out of my way." Ugh. Gino and Hathoway were listening. Down there, somewhere. Witnessing my weakness. *Suck it up, girl!* "I just need some room to maneuver. Don't want to smash you in that pretty face of yours, Super Agent Man. Now, move … please."

Fragile bravado. It was the best I could muster.

Theater in the wood. I'd done my part. What role would Nick choose to play? He lifted his hand from my leg and jumped down, cat-like, landing on all fours in the thick, damp leaves before pushing to his feet and stepping away.

Thank you. Was it enough to keep my pride in tact in front of a relative stranger? Hathoway busied himself by marking off spots for the perimeter tape. If he'd seen or heard anything between us, he wasn't letting on. *God bless him.*

Gino'd seen and heard enough over the years. Now I could save time rehashing the details when we inevitably sat down to talk about it.

Faces appeared through the foliage. Four men in FBI jackets emerged out of the woods and stood beside Nick. His cavalry had arrived.

I let out a long breath and resumed my descent. Foot by foot, hand under hand. One last rustic step, and Gino's arms circled my waist as I dropped to the forest floor beneath the monstrous tree house. And the body.

I turned around to face him. Where had Nick wandered off to?

"She was strung up like a deer, G. And she was wearing a mask. McCaskey was right." My voice was an iron fist. "I'm gonna kill that witch. I swear, I am." My words sliced the air like a burst of machine gun fire.

Gino's arms pulled me into a life-giving hug. "Shush, m'hija. We will not do God's work for Him. Rather, we will let Him do His work through us. He says, 'Vengeance is mine.'"

Huh. A God into justice. That was some theology I could relate to.

CHAPTER FORTY-SIX

Saturday, March 26

Gino and I walked back to the road in silence, arms linked. Hathoway and Nick remained behind with the team, securing and processing the scene. By the time we reached the road, dark sedans rushed down the highway toward us, lights flashing.

"Looks like quite a crowd is gathering." I nudged Gino. "Nothing I want to stick around here for. Let's get back to the station. See what we can do. Or see." Thick, steel bands wrapped around my shoulders.

"I have a better idea." He opened the passenger door for me before walking around and sliding into the driver's seat. I placed Nick's smart key in Gino's hand, squeezing it hard before letting it go.

"Shoot." I rubbed my eyes.

"I take you home." He raised his hand to me, patted the air. "Do not object. You are too tired, and you have seen too much. There is nothing we can do for the moment. Trust that our Nick can clear a crime scene and that he and Commander Mitchell can write up a report. Let us take care of that little bit for you, m'hija." He tipped my chin up.

I looked into his soft brown eyes. He was right. "I am exhausted. A shower and a nap would do me a world of good. And then I'll look in on my mom, and we'll go catch us one bad cat. Before she kills again."

"You do recall we have posted guards 'round the clock at your mother's hospital room door, yes?" Gino's hand trailed down to his seatbelt, buckling it.

"Yes. I know she's safe. And I know there's nothing else we can do, but that doesn't mean I don't hate every second of sitting around. The vulnerability. The uselessness of it all." I rubbed my temples.

"Still, even the useless ones need to rest, m'hija." Gino winked at me, like a Cuban Santa, and I started to laugh.

"*¡Basta!* You win, amigo mio. Take me home already." I grabbed his hand and squeezed. Maybe he could feel the gratitude flowing from my heart to his.

"And on the way, you can forget about la mala long enough to tell me what it is that has gotten into you to be treating our St. Nicholas *con tanta fría*." He pushed the start button, and the engine roared to life.

"What are you talking about?" *Might as well feign ignorance. To start.*

He shook his head with a grunt and steered the SUV onto the country highway. "I could as easily have died from frostbite sitting near you two as I could from triggering explosives planted in the woods."

Two more sedans and an ambulance, lights flashing, no sirens, zoomed past us in the opposite lane.

"It's … I can explain …" I fidgeted in my seat, running my hand up and down the shoulder harness.

"Uh-huh." He flashed a crooked smile in my direction as he drove. "A glacier warms the soul more than your way of looking at the man I thought you loved."

I couldn't even argue his point. "I, uh, it's hard to put into so many words."

"Is it really, Josephine? Is it words? Or is it fear?" The radio crackled. Gino stopped midsentence and turned it up.

Nick's voice came on. "G, you copy?"

"*Venga, hermano.*" Gino answered in a flash. *C'mon, brother.*

"Get her home safe for me, will you?" Tenderness, encased in sorrow.

Gino nodded. "*Te prometo.* I will care for her as fiercely as you would, old friend. Go with the protection of our God."

He ended the call and turned to look at me as he drove.

"St. Nicolas even now wishes only to protect you. Why would a woman refuse such a love as this?"

I had a better question, but I kept it to myself. Which would be worse, continuing to push a good man away, or risking everything for a chance at something real … and losing it?

CHAPTER FORTY-SEVEN

Saturday, March 26

The automatic porch lights were on when Gino pulled into my driveway. My eyes wandered to Donna and Jim's house next door. Porch lights on, house lights off. Must've gone out for the evening.

Gino scrolled through the messages on his cell. "Will you be alright for a few hours, m'hija? There have been some more problems with the tracking equipment I must tend to. But it could perhaps wait."

It seemed more a request than a question. Gino needed rest as much as I did. Maybe even more.

"Go. And know how much I appreciate you, G." I half hugged him over the front seat, kissed his cheek, and slid out onto the pavement.

I gave a weak wave as he backed down the driveway, then trudged up the steps to my front door. The sky rumbled overhead. Signs of yet another spring shower on the way sprang across the sky in quick flashes, followed long seconds after by muted thunder. Perfect sleeping weather. I'd be snoring by eight p.m.

A slip of paper was jammed between the screen door and the frame. I snatched it out and turned it over, squinting at the small but elegant scrawl I knew so well.

Josie, we're heading to Lake Geneva for the night. The dogs insisted on spending the night with you—hope you don't mind. Love you.

I smiled and opened the front door, alerting the two Brittany spaniels to my presence. Lennie and Lexie bounded to the door, barking as if they'd treed something big. Taking care of them might be just the therapy I'd need to give myself permission to tend to my own needs.

I sank to my knees in the foyer, talking to them each in turn. Their sleek coats drained the tension that had consumed me for the past several hours. Good grief, the amount of tragedy and mystery that had occurred since I'd gotten out of bed that morning was ridiculous. And I didn't want to think about it anymore.

Was there enough time to get the dogs out for a quick walk before the rain started in for good? Lightning lit up the sky outside the windows at random intervals, sending both dogs into nervous fits of barking. I parted the curtains. A pillar of angry clouds hung low in front of the house.

We'll let this blow over, go outside later. I could've killed for a shower, but after settling the dogs in with food and water, I tossed myself onto the sofa like an old blanket, falling asleep the minute my head hit the cushion.

Sharp barks pulled me out of my slumber. Lennie and Lexie were pacing and barking feverishly. How long had I been asleep? There was a deeper sound piercing the night than their barking. Rain bulleted the roof, and gale-force winds rammed the house with ghastly shrieks and groans. Something thumped against the wall next to the couch. Lawn furniture?

The low sound bleated again. The town's tornado siren. How long had that been going off? Another whomp against the house. Lennie and Lexie nosed my legs, urging me to my feet. I grabbed a flashlight from the kitchen junk drawer, dogs on either side of me. Dragging sounds fluttered around me right before the trilling of breaking glass. Another round of lightning sizzled across the sky, immediately chased by peals of thunder, sending me scurrying toward the basement steps.

The dogs clambered after me. Lennie hesitated as I rounded the corner and headed down. Lexie froze behind him. Dang! They hadn't been down there before. I stepped back up and grabbed Lennie's collar. Maybe Lexie would follow.

"C'mon! Move!" I spat at them like a madwoman, patting Lennie's head and tugging his collar, before resorting to pushing him down the stairs ahead of me with my foot while dragging Lexie behind me by the collar. The flashlight knocked against her head twice, but it couldn't be helped. She barked out her response. Lennie started answering.

Another violent crack of lightning lit up and shook the house. Mighty roars of wind drowned out their barking as we scuttled down the stairs.

A sense of home hit me when my feet touched the cement of the basement landing. Teeth rubbed against the back of my hand as I pushed through the door, but the roaring and the shaking of the house demanded my attention. The lights flickered once before going out and plunging us into darkness. I switched on the flashlight.

The door slammed behind us, and I fell against it, breathing hard, speaking to the dogs in soothing tones. "It's alright … it's alright … you're okay. You don't need to cry anymore."

Both dogs yelped in response, their frantic eyes locked on mine. Overhead, crashing sounds continued. What was happening up there? Another wallop sent the house shuddering as if a giant had taken a bulldozer to it, stirring the dogs up into a new frenzy. I pulled them both into an alcove behind the stairwell, well away from any windows. The pulling turned into dragging.

"Shush! C'mere guys." I did my best to find low soothing tones, but they ignored me, barking non-stop. Lennie was even foaming a little. Then, they both leapt to their feet and circled in front of me, growling.

"Enough! *No!* Quiet!" They returned to barking, now at a fever pitch as a blast of hot air slapped across my face. "Are we on fire?" I crab-walked over to the basement door—it was warm to my touch. I worked my hand carefully up the hollow door. I jerked it away halfway up and shook it rapidly. Fire!

We're trapped. Smoke poured under the door. I started coughing and looking around the room through the warm haze. There had to be something I could do, but I had to be fast. Cast iron kitchen stools, long ago out of date, lined the basement wall. *Perfect.*

They were heavy, and my back was sore from the crazy hours behind me. *Please be with me, God. Go before me.* I strained to heave one up over my shoulder and fast-walk to the window well. When I got within two feet of it, I used every ounce of energy I could muster and slammed the heavy stool against the window. Nothing—not a crack, not a scratch. I drew the stool back and tried again. Still, the window held. Smoke curled in layers around my feet, and Lexie started howling like a soulful coyote.

Lennie yipped and snapped at my cloudy ankles, shaking drool every which way as he gave himself over entirely to primal fear. "Lennie, no!"

He emitted a high pitched yelp right before charging me. I hit him in the side of the head with my fist as he lunged.

"We've got to get out of here!" If the fire didn't kill me, Lennie might. I looked around again, pointing the flashlight beam up and down each wall. *God! I need you!* Half a dozen field stones from a garden project long forgotten glinted on a shelf on the opposite wall. I ran to the shelf, grabbed a medium sized quartz stone, ran back to the window, and flung it as hard as I could.

The stone clattered off the window, leaving a small crack along the base. I picked up the stone with both hands, backed up a few steps, lifted it over my head and shot-putted the thing. The stone hit the lower middle of the window and landed in the gravel on the other side, sending shards of broken glass to the floor. *Thank you, God!*

I staggered back to the heavy stool and used it to knock out the jagged glass, eerily reminiscent of what I'd done only a few hours before. I coughed and gasped as the smoke billowed into the room with the lure of fresh air.

"Lennie, come! C'mere, Lexie!" Both crazed animals stood a few feet behind me. Lennie was still wild eyed. I grabbed Lexie first, pushed her through the jagged glass opening onto the damp earth of the basement window well. Good enough for now.

I snatched a lamp from the floor and wrenched the cord, breaking it off at the base. Then I dragged the heavy stool over to the window. Lennie was panting, holding one front paw up. His eyes rolled back, and I took my chance. I dove at him, wrapped the cord twice around his muzzle and once around his neck, and fireman carried him over to the stool.

Help me hold on just a little longer, God! Get us through this! I put Lennie on the stool first, then climbed up the rung and put my left foot next to his body. He didn't move. Maybe he was in shock, but it worked. I grabbed him by the collar, struggling to get his hips into my arms. He started growling as I slipped my hands under his hips, and then he tried to open his jaws. The cord gave, and he bit me, right on the neck. I screamed and threw him through the window and onto the damp earth next to Lexie, where he got to his feet and started barking again.

Drained, I hoisted myself up onto the iron stool and pushed myself through the window, scraping my back on protruding glass shards for the second time that day. Warm blood drizzled its way down my back as I squirmed through. I knelt in the window well, surrounded by furry legs, muddy ground, and hailstones. I tried to push myself up, but my shaky thighs wouldn't move. Spaghetti arms flailed through a dark tunnel right before my cheek fell hard against the mud.

Lexie licked my face. A voice called to me from within. *Get up. Get up, Jo.* I obeyed. Heat rose around me, and I looked up. My house was a blazing inferno. It burned, wild flames bursting through the roof, through every window on the first and second floor, unrelenting in the pouring rain and hail. Flames licked my hair, and I crouched low.

I grabbed Lennie one last time, heaved him up the four feet of warm steel window well, and tossed him as far as I could. Then, I did the same with Lexie. Both dogs circled back to me, confused in their new-found freedom, crazed. I felt the sides of the window well. It was growing warmer, but I could do it—I had to do it. *Please be with me, God. Give me one last ounce of strength.*

On three. I gripped the steaming metal with both hands and pushed myself up onto the side of the window well. My abs hit the hot steel, and I cried out, but I kept pushing until I was free. My stomach, thighs, and hips burned in agony, begging me to give up and lie still. But I listened to another voice, pulling myself out onto the wet grass. I pushed myself up with blistered hands and half jogged, half ran into the tall wet prairie grass that grew between homes on my street, chased by Lennie and Lexie, singed and smelly … but alive. An eerie calm filled the air.

Strong hands gripped my shoulders, and I was maneuvered along the wet path toward a bright light, while the cold rain pounded. Surrounded by a cacophony of sounds—chirping, screaming, barking, roaring … so many sounds … so many people … Where did they all come from? Armies of black-cloaked beasts with hoses and bright, bright lights loomed before me … in the midst of all of the screams, sirens, and chaotic sounds, the chirping continued.

The sound was coming from my pocket. I dug into the remnants of my pants pocket, pulled my cell phone out, and pressed it against my ear. A sultry voice broke through the clamor of noise. "Hot enough for you now?"

CHAPTER FORTY-EIGHT

Sunday, March 27

Fluffy clouds of pink, green, and blue floated past. Sam and I, eating cotton candy, hand in hand, laughing and walking through midway of the Sauk County Fair.

My eyelids, sewn shut with sleep, opened lash by lash and revealed a large shape next to the bed—fuzzy, shaggy-headed. Warmth like a puppy squirmed in my hand, caressing my fingers, little kisses moving from tip to tip. I smiled, giggling at the sensations, the warmth, the life flowing through me.

"Hello, beautiful." Nick's golden voice. Nick. At my bedside, holding my hand to his glorious lips. Nick to the rescue.

Nick. Always and ever Nick. *His* were the strong arms that led me to safety, away from the fire. How had he known to come find me? How did he always seem to be in the right place at the right time? I didn't believe in divine appointments, did I? Maybe Nick was … maybe I should …

Cold marble slabs boxed in my heart. My tongue stuck itself to the roof of my mouth. The giddy incertitude of the hospital-strength painkillers wore off. Nick was killing my buzz. With his love. What did that say about me?

My world-weary eyes found his. Deep brown pools of adoration and steady promises stared out at me from an impossibly handsome face, custom-stitched together in love. For me. For us. Did I deserve an 'us' with him? Did I even want it?

That was it.

The root of my fear—I didn't deserve him. I wasn't good enough for him. Between my horrible marriage and drama-laden life, how could he love me? If and when he saw the real me, the me behind the tough-girl mask I always wore, he'd bolt. He'd leave me. Just like Del. It was a risk I couldn't take; a belief I couldn't confront. Shame burned across my face, dragged my eyes away from his, severing the connection between us.

"Nick … I can't." I shook my head, eyes burning, my skin clammy. Maybe he would read the finality in my tone, in the sad turn of my head. In the words I couldn't speak. In the shame I couldn't escape, couldn't outrun, couldn't kill. My fear was a love-sucking zombie, and I was out of ammo. At the worst possible time. Surrounded by Nick's love, unable to put my fears to death. Unable to move ahead, too scared to step back.

"Josie, I don't care what's in your head. I know what's in your heart. And I'm a patient man. I can wait for you to face your fears." He kept his steady eyes on me and traced the layers of gauze on my blistered palm with his finger.

My hand was numb. Drugs? Or fear? *Petrified in place.* I shook my head, kept my eyes trained on the wall behind him. *Come on, Nick, get the message, walk away, don't tease me any more with a love that can't last.*

He rose, scooted the chair closer to the bed, and sat back down, leaning in. I flinched. He drew back, fished in his jacket, pulled out a picture, and placed it next to a vase of Easter lilies on the table next to the bed. Easter … my favorite holiday. Was it today? I still didn't have my holiday china. In the photo, Sam smiled down at me, nestled in my arms, Nick's arms around us both. That had been a perfect day together. The warmth of the memory was better than a chocolate bunny.

He persevered. "I need you to know a few things, and then I'll give you some time alone. I'm telling you now, and I'll tell you again when you're out of this place and back on your feet—fighting the world, fighting me. But, Josie, you don't need to fight me. Not now, not ever." He brushed my bangs out of my eyes, trailed his finger over my lips.

The "Hallelujah Chorus" sounded in my heart. Moments later, I was a country under siege. I loved his touch. My tears threatened to ruin another perfect moment between us.

I moved my head away.

He kissed the top of my head and cupped my face in his hands. "I love you. Whatever this is, this push-me-pull-you thing you've got going on, is not from me. And, maybe more importantly, it's not from God. 'God is not a God of confusion, but of peace.'"

He picked my hand up again. "And I have the deepest peace. About me … and about you. But here's one thing I know—God is bigger than my need for you. Believe me, this is not a man saying this in his own power, because I need you more than life itself. But my God is bigger, even bigger than my love. And He's given me an abiding peace about you. About Sam. About us."

He sighed, sorrow creeping into his voice. "I can see and feel you trying to sabotage this relationship. But I'm here to tell you, beautiful— that can't be done."

He took a deep breath and let it out. "I'm a good man, a man who loves you, loves our little Samantha, and loves the God who stands behind you both. And I. Can. Wait. For. You." He kissed my hand, his lips feather soft and damp. A tear? "And I will."

Commitment resonated through his words. "So hear me, Jo Oliver. I'm taking a step back from you, from us. Because even I recognize this isn't our time. But I need *you* to recognize this: our time will come. And I'll leave that up to you and God."

What? Was he leaving me behind?

Wasn't that what I said I wanted? My guts churned through the soft morphine haze.

Amusement danced in his eyes. He leaned in, his lips close to my ear. "Hey, hey, hey! Don't cry, beautiful! I'll be back. Look, here's how you can know."

He leaned away from me and stood up, rummaging around in his pockets. He found what he was after and bent back to the bed, pressing something cold and hard into my hand.

I looked up into gorgeous eyes and found an ocean of love and longing. And a smirk.

"That's right. My prized possession is now in *your* possession. And you know I'll want it back. What could possibly be more important to a man than his Leatherman?" He winked at me, inviting me into the warmth of him—the truth of him.

He was a wonderful man. A solid man. Any other woman would kill to be in my position. Kira literally had killed to be in my position. I just held tight onto his Leatherman, blinking back tears in silence.

"All I ask is that you bring your fears into the light. Remember, God is not a God of fear. But of peace and of power. Do you hear me? Our God is a God of love. And perfect love casts out fear. That's what I want for us—a perfect love."

He kissed my ear, kissed my cheek. Kissed away a salty tear shed as the beauty of his words filleted me. "So I'll stand back, but not down. To give God room to soften the edge of your fear. And help you put it down. That's my prayer for you."

And with that, he kissed my hand again, and stepped out of the room.

I lay in the bed, swarming with emotion. Then I pressed the button on the morphine pump. Hard.

CHAPTER FORTY-NINE

Sunday, March 27

Elephants in tutus and merchants in top hats marched up and down the dirt roads of a Wild West set. I forced my eyes open just as a giant boa constrictor's wide-open jaws scratched the top of my head. My reward was the ceiling's gentle swaying. Then it ratcheted up to out-of-control carousel speed, and I shut my eyes tight.

I sucked in air until my lungs ached. *God? Remember me? Are You up there?* The long, slow exhalation spread drowsiness down my body. I squeezed Nick's Leatherman, its hard steel edges and the contrasting warmth of its leather-wrapped handle.

Large, dark swans swooped low overhead. Graceful, otherworldly, foreboding. The most beautiful of the swans fell away from the head of the formation and dove straight toward me. The beauty disintegrated into evil. Its beak turned into the vicious jaws of a great white shark. I lay there, paralyzed, while the threat careened toward me. It was less than ten feet away when I woke up.

The graceful swan loomed over me. I shook my head, blinked, and looked again at the apparition. Scrubs, hair pulled back—it was a tall nurse with dark hair. I couldn't make out the nametag, but I knew her, didn't I? There was something about her face. Something dark and alarming.

She looked down at me with a sneer, her lips moving. What was she saying?

Focus, Josie, focus. I closed my eyes once more, shook my head twice, and opened them again. The smooth flow of the IV drip wavered out of focus, and the lithe figure etched in white against the gray-walled backdrop of the room came into view. Her face was shining, her eyes were dark, and she held a needle in her hand.

Through the smog of morphine, I looked right at her and laughed. Dressed as a cartoon-like nurse, looming large and threatening me with an oversized needle, was hilarious.

Kira, however, was not amused.

Black rage covered her features, and the needle started to tremble. My eyes widened, but I couldn't hold back the laughter. This was all wrong, and that made it seem even funnier. Her enraged face seemed to swell as she stood over me.

She pushed the plunger on the hypodermic needle to squeeze out any air.

"Wh, why bodder if you gonna kill me anyway?" My tongue wasn't working. I couldn't get the words out straight.

Her head shook angrily as she flicked the tip of the needle with the end of her middle finger. She cocked an eyebrow, staring down at me in surprise. "You're drunk. How quaint."

She smiled tightly while her eyes raged on.

She was going to kill me. This was it. Her one wide-open shot at getting the scopolamine overdose into my system in a way that no one would ever suspect. I'd die without a fuss, without a whimper. Without a witness. Would it hurt? Would I even feel it?

Nick's face floated across the room, and I smiled. And then the deepest sense of peace I'd ever known fell all around me like a protective shield. My heart turned to Heaven and something in me shifted. *Nick. I want Nick.*

Kira's contorted face wobbled over my bed. Her lips were still moving. She was taunting me, but her words came out as gibberish to my glazed brain. Her voice rose, and she jabbed the needle in the air, emphasizing some point.

I shrank back in my bed. Nick. His staunch declaration of love and patience, standing up next to the truth as it wound its way through the hazy spindles of my mind. The picture of the three of us, nestled happily in each other's arms, burst through my haze in Technicolor. I wanted to live. To love. To wrap my arms around the three of us and never let go.

My right hand was wrapped around something flat, with sharp edges. A flashdrive? *Too big.* My cell phone? *Too small.* I clenched my fist again, sharp tines digging into my hand. Utensil of some kind. *The Leatherman!*

Nick's special-order Leatherman with the illegal switchblade. *Makes it easier to fillet a fish.* He was so proud of another of Gino's uniquely adjusted, repurposed gifts. My thumb roved over the handle, finding the round indentation. Gotcha.

Kira's soliloquy continued. I turned my head from side to side and kept my eyes down, signifying defeat. She raised her voice and soldiered on. Every other word was a curse. She wasn't very happy I was alive. And she had every intention of fixing that very soon.

I squeezed out a few tears and looked up at her. *Keep talking, Kira.* She rewarded me with a fresh onslaught. I edged my right hand down my thigh, just under the edge of the sheet to conceal it. Then I coughed and pressed the button. The thin blade swooshed out, ready for action.

Forcing more fake tears out, I gave her what satisfaction I could, buying more time. I squinted as if in fear, judging the distance. *Closer. I need to get her closer.*

She was still talking, still gloating. "You think you've stopped me? Once your death hits our pathetic Nick, I win. It's as good as killing both of you. Better."

She stared at me and leaned in. My eyes opened wide as if in fear, and she smiled. I willed my dry lips to move, managed enough energy to smirk, but not open my mouth.

A spark of surprise flashed through her eyes, and she bent down to hear what I was trying to say. I slipped the blade from beneath the covers and eased my hand up to my hip, hovering an inch above the bed. Come closer. Then I concentrated on moving my lips. I clenched my stomach, forcing air up, and whispered to her. "Kira, what …"

Hearing her name seemed to please her. She bent her knees and drew closer, hooking her thumb over the bed frame, still holding the syringe. I moved my lips again, luring her in while dragging the Leatherman up another two inches, fully in position. It was now or never.

I thrust that thing in her belly, twisting and ripping like I was eviscerating a pig. Blood shot out over me. Her intestines spilled out, but I kept the pressure on the blade. She fell onto me, mouth opening and closing, wildly slashing the air with the scopolamine-filled needle. My free hand scrambled to find the call button, and I pressed down.

I did my best to pull the blade back, but the weight of her body and gravity teamed up against me. In the end, I inched it out as far as I could, and held on to Nick's Leatherman like a talisman. A river of warmth flowed over my body. Was she bleeding out?

Please don't let her die, God.

Did I want her to live? I needed her to live, to account for her crimes. Provide some closure for the victims' families.

The wedge of swans returned. White ones and black ones, of all shapes and sizes. Some were honking—others wore grim silence like a badge. No, not *like* badges. They wore badges. A bag of cement was lifted from my body. Cold, wet, sticky rolls of paper were left behind. I wanted them off, but I was unable to move. Had she plunged the scopolamine in before she fell?

Hands pulled at my fingers. What did they want from me now? Why wouldn't they all fly away? Ah. The knife. They wanted the Leatherman. Well, they couldn't have it.

Some women wanted diamonds. I clenched my fingers tighter around Nick's Leatherman and smiled. He'd already given me everything I wanted, everything I needed. It might have been the drugs, but that strong, soothing sense of peace permeated me as I rode the current up into the air and floated away on swan's wings.

THANK YOU!

I hope you enjoyed reading *Shattered by Death* as much as I enjoyed writing it! Please consider sharing your thoughts on this and other recent reads via an honest review on Amazon or Goodreads.

Your input means the world to writers and your recommendations to friends and on social media have the power to make or break our books.

Thank you so much for reading *Shattered by Death* and for spending time with me.

In gratitude,

Catherine Finger

DISCUSSION QUESTIONS

Jo Oliver struggles with her faith. Gino serves as her spiritual mentor. What faith struggles do you experience? Who do you turn to when you need to work through your faith issues?

How does Jo Oliver cope with the pain of betrayal in her life? Do you think she works to avoiding feeling pain? What do you do to avoid feeling pain? What can you do to begin growing through that area of your life?

Part of Jo's journey has to do with reconciliation with her past, and with her faith. What does she do to make peace with her past and what part does her faith play in this process?

Jo Oliver is a strong female leader in a man's world. Does she face gender discrimination? What examples support your response?

Do you think the portrayal of Jo Oliver as a female police chief is realistic? Why or why not?

Jo Oliver's struggle to become a mother to Samantha is a constant theme. What are some of her fears related to motherhood? How does she overcome them? Do these fears resonate with your own experience?

The tension between Jo and Nick ebbs and flows, as do Jo's feelings toward him. Why do you think she is so ambivalent about his role in her life? How do you think she really feels about him? What do you think she really wants?

Have you ever felt extreme ambivalence in a relationship? How did you handle it?

Justice is an underlying theme throughout Shattered by Death. At one point, Kira suggests that some people deserve to die. Do you think doing what is clearly the wrong thing is ever justified?

Jo Oliver has built a strong network of caring friends who stand by her in the midst of difficult circumstances. What do you see her doing to nurture her relationships with others? What do you do to keep your own personal sense of community strong?

ABOUT THE AUTHOR

CATHERINE FINGER loves to dream, write, and tell stories. Recently retired from a wonderful career in public education, she celebrates the ability to choose how to spend her time in a new way during the second half of life. So far, she chooses to write books, ride horses, serve others, and generally find her way into and out of trouble both on the road and at home. She lives in the Midwest with a warm and wonderful combination of family and friends .

Anchored by Death (Elk Lake Publishing, Inc) the third novel in her Jo Oliver Thriller series, received the Bronze Medal for the 2018 Independent Publisher Book Awards. Her second Jo Oliver Thriller, *Shattered by Death* (Elk Lake Publishing, Inc) was named 2016 Book of the Year by Deep River Books and was a finalist in both the International Book Awards and the National Indie Excellence Awards. Catherine and her novels have been featured on radio stations, blogs, and in numerous articles—all posted at www. CatherineFinger.com.

Catherine loves to interact with her readers at www.CatherineFinger. com Follow her on Facebook at Catherine Finger, Author, and on Twitter at CatherineFinger@BeJoOliver

www.ingramcontent.com/pod-product-compliance
Lightning Source LLC
Chambersburg PA
CBHW072052170626
46813CB00004B/1311